THE FALSE AND THE UNFAIR

A Novel

Roger Armbrust

Crossbow Press

To Ted Parkhurst, dear friend who for decades believed in my writing and published it.

To Allen Alverson,

with Blessings.

Rosa Ramy A

6-18-25

Yes,   *the*   *fight*
Against   *the*   *false*   *and*   *the*   *unfair*
Was always worth it.

W.H. AUDEN
FROM HIS POEM "VOLTAIRE AT FERNEY"

CONTENTS

AN EXPLOSIVE DOCUMENT

"The journalist never assumes."

Mitchell Morgan these years later still could hear his college teacher's voice in that first class. He eventually realized that dictum related to EVERYTHING. Down to proofreading his own byline when reviewing the newspaper's layout.

So here again, on Tuesday's deadline night, he was doing that right now on *Center Stage*'s front-page lead story. The headline, subhead, then byline:

SAG-AFTRA VOTES TO STRIKE SPOT PRODUCERS

Union will begin picketing commercial shoots on Wednesday

By Mitchell Morgan

SAG was the Screen Actors Guild. AFTRA the American Federation of Television and Radio Artists. The two separate performers unions had merged in 2012. Now in 2030, their over 300,000-strong organization – film, TV, radio, and streaming-production performers primarily in New York, Los Angeles, Chicago, and smaller cities nationwide – had agreed to walk off any current commercial productions and begin picketing production sites and commercial producers' national and regional headquarters.

In his over 10 years as national news editor at *Center Stage*, Mitchell had seen strikes before. They were never pretty. Actors were the bottom of the production food chain, easy to abuse because of their dedication to their crafts, their artistic insecurity, and financial instability due to their vast numbers competing to get into limited scheduled shoots. It meant only a small percentage of union members actually made living annual wages while many had to work parttime jobs in order to survive while auditioning for acting chances.

The bottom line: a strike meant no work, only picketing. No work meant no money. If the strike lasted a month or more, actors would get hungry, very hungry. And start to become angry. The union's strike fund might help a little, but only a little. And a little didn't go far in big cities, covering maybe 10 percent of an actor's average income.

Mitchell recalled how the last strike, on feature film productions, had dragged on for six months. Anger had turned to some scattered incidences of violence, ranging from fistfights between union members and scabs on an active shoot to a couple of bomb scares. But those were fortunately minor occurrences, primarily because film stars – who make or break a motion picture – are all union members, once hungry actors who made it. And the film stars all honored the strike, basically freezing all major feature film production.

The new commercial film production strike was a different animal with a different contract, and yet subject to the same obstacles, from a producer's point of view. Most commercials didn't rely on film stars. They used mainly unknown actors paid salaries based on the union-negotiated commercials pact. But they would be striking, as would feature actors who performed in commercials. However, some commercial producers might try to sneak in scabs to complete their projects, and that could be dangerous if hungry and angry union members caught them.

Mitchell had explained all this in his lead story. His final read found that the proofreaders had done a good job with corrections, and he had changed back a couple of alterations in which a proofreader had gotten out of line, thinking he was an editor, challenging Mitchell's phrasing.

It was nearing midnight, and the paper needed to close on deadline, waiting only on final changes to the classified pages. Derrick Hanley, the layout editor, was struggling with those.

Mitchell moved across the editorial floor to Derrick's cubicle.

"How are the final classifieds coming?" he asked.

"I got it. I got it," Derrick mumbled, his red face indicating he didn't have it. "It won't be long."

They would be able to close just after 2 a.m., when Derrick finally got it. Unfortunately for him, but not for the paper, he wouldn't have to get it very much longer. Within a month, he'd be let go.

It was easy for the paper to let him and anyone else go. Although *Center Stage*'s mission and profit motive was reporting on performers' unions, and selling ads announcing audition openings to productions, it insured the owners' profit motive by blocking any effort at unionizing the paper itself.

The newspaper, in fact corporations nationwide, in the '90s had stabilized a nonunion effort through their hiring practices and management appointments. They had begun firing full-time workers to end their salaries and benefits, then would hire them back part-time to perform the same job functions. Facing a strangle-tight labor market, workers had little choice but to take the offers and return to the stubborn corporations.

Center Stage had seen cases of that over the years, and still relied heavily on freelance writers, with a handful of full-time editors, all with management titles like Mitch's. With only "managers", there were no full-time employees who could form a union.

Meanwhile, the full-time editors had taken on additional responsibilities when the paper decided, like most publications, to dedicate more time and money to expanding Internet publishing.

Editing had gone from simply a Tuesday night deadline, which still existed for the weekly print edition, to daily constant "filling the buckets": incessantly updating the online newspaper's many sections ranging from film and commercial production news to Broadway

4

and Off-Broadway and Off-Off-Broadway stories, to union news, to national, state, and local government funding of the arts.

Arts funding was the life-source for non-profit theater, particularly in New York, LA, and Chicago. And those theaters provided acting work which, although it didn't pay actors, it did provide a literal stage where they could be seen by agents and producers. And struggling playwrights would have chances for their new works to be produced.

Mitchell had finished reviewing the print edition's news stories just after midnight, and was reflecting on all this when his phone rang.

"Mitchell Morgan."

"Shing me a shong," the slurry female voice mumbled.

"Have you been drinking?"

"Jush a bit…one or two…"

Mitchell and Rachel had lived together for two years. With twenty years of sobriety, he had avoided getting involved with a sober woman, concerned that two addictive personalities under one roof might lead to a Tennessee Williams drama rather than an honest, caring relationship. But his first sight of Rachel, her raven hair, sky-blue eyes, and starlet's presence had changed all that. He saw her at a recovery meeting, and he fell. They had coffee after. They began dating. Her being over five years sober, and the seeming firm foundation that came with it, led him to relent. And her too.

She was a respected book editor at a major publishing house, but in the last month had begun feeling pressure there, as well as suffering from distant disgruntled small-town family ties. And she had begun neglecting the regular meetings that stabilize an alcoholic's sobriety.

So it looked like tonight she had decided to invite the devil in.

"I don't have time for this," Mitch snapped. "I should be home in a couple of hours."

"Ohhh…bitchy Mitchy…comin' home late…I might not be here…" Click.

Larry Cohen, the national theatre editor, was standing next to Mitch's desk.

"Mitch, have you talked to Derrick?" Larry sighed. "When are we getting out of here?"

"New York, New York," Mitch responded, cracking a grin, singing lightly. "If I can make it there, I'll make it anywhere."

Then Larry joined him:

"It's up to YOU! New York, New York!"

They both walked back to the corporate kitchen to refresh the decaf.

The January night breathed a deep chill into Mitch as he walked out onto Ninth Street, moving the half-block west to lower Broadway. The city may have been sleepless, but it was yawning, the winter wind and threat of snow chasing folks inside.

He moved down to Fourth Street, continued west past New York University's library on his left, Washington Square Park on his right.

Turning left at the library's corner, he looked up. The bitter cold wind had cleared the smog and cloud-cover, presenting a brief pristine night sky. There was Orion. So rare to see, Mitchell actually stopped, stared at the constellation, and breathed a soft, "Heyyy...Hi!"

He thought about it twinkling back, just at him. Then he sniffed a laugh and headed home as cloud cover quickly banished the heavens.

The small Greenwich Village apartment was dark and silent as he opened and quietly shut the door, clicking the three locks. He stepped left into the living/writing room, turned on the desk lamp. No Rachel passed out on the couch. He looked right past the recessed kitchenette to the open bedroom. No Rachel on the futon. Nor in the bathroom.

He opened the expanded shuttered doors of the closet. No Rachel's clothes or suitcase. He sat on the futon, sighed and thought.

6

"Please, Great Spirit, keep her safe from this miserable night," he whispered.

He looked out the window. Snow had begun to fall, not gently like a Christmas movie, but heavy like a horror film.

Exhausted, he lay out prone on the bed, toed off his Skechers running shoes, and began deep-breathing to relax. Hopefully she had taken a cab to Monica's, her usual haven when she wanted both sympathy and straight talk from a real friend.

He mumbled a prayer of thanks that he was sober, that she would please get to a meeting Wednesday. It helped him drift into sleep, full-clothed.

The snow had proved relentless through the night. By the time Mitch stepped beyond the apartments' courtyard onto Sullivan Street, the sun had broken through, but the temperature had fallen to near zero, assuring the white crust would hold firm.

The snowplows had cleared the streets for traffic, but no one had shoveled the sidewalks. So Mitch found it easier walking on the street's edge between slow-moving car/truck flow and snow plowed next to the curb, the long white wall thigh high.

Mitch stopped in at the McDonald's on Broadway to grab a quick breakfast. Seated at one of the small tables among the rustling crowd, he munched quickly on a sausage-and-egg McMuffin, sipping his iced Coke (a habit even in winter), and opened the folded copy of *Center Stage* he had brought with him. His chance to give it a scan with fresh eyes.

He noticed a figure moving to his table and taking a seat across from him, setting down his tray, and a couple of papers and magazines. A common occurrence in Manhattan where fast-foods are constantly crowded, forcing strangers to sit across from each other.

In his journalist's habit, Mitch glanced at the papers and magazines the man had laid down. *The New York Times*, *Wall Street Journal*, a magazine called *Security Week*, and a mag beneath it with a hidden masthead except for the tops of three letters which looked like S-P-Y.

He looked up to see a ruggedly handsome middle-aged man with a Neanderthal square head and pug nose and bit of a pockmarked complexion. He had only coffee, and seemed to look out in slight confusion, as if questioning himself.

Mitch began looking over *Center Stage*'s front page, then homed in on his own article. Half-way through, he breathed out a soft "Oh, fuck."

"Your team lose?"

The man across the table was watching him with slightly bloodshot amber eyes, a small brief smile quickly returning to a serious expression.

Mitch grinned slightly, shaking his head.

"Naw. This article I wrote has a terrible typo. I didn't catch it. Neither did the proofreader."

"You're a journalist?"

"Yeah, but worse than that. I'm an editor who missed a pretty embarrassing screw-up in my own piece."

The man winced as if waiting for more information.

"I interviewed the head of a union and asked if they had voted to strike. He answered 'You betcha!' The computer evidently decided to do its own edit. Changed his answer to 'You bitch.' So he seems to be suddenly cussing and making no sense. I'll need to call him when I get to work, and get tech to make the change on the website so the article will be correct for the online readers."

The man nodded as if he understood, but his eyes were gazing around in that same earlier confused expression. He stayed quiet.

Mitch studied him. "What do you do?"

He kept glancing around at their surroundings, uneasy.

"I'm…retired."

"Wow. You look pretty young to be retired. What? Did you sell your digital company to a giant like Omicron?"

The man continued to gaze out, confused. Mitch's journalistic instinct led him to look down closer at the man's top paper. The mailing sticker on it read

Wilmer Bracken

332 E. Houston St., Apt. 412

New York, NY 10002

"No," he finally responded. "I worked…for…our government."

"What? City Hall?"

"No…for…the federal…government."

"Please tell me not the IRS," Mitch said jokingly.

The man didn't smile. He looked down as if searching for the right words.

"The…yes…the CIA."

Mitch sat quietly, not sure how to respond to that.

"Yes…the CIA," he repeated, as if struggling to assure himself. He looked up with a pained expression and straight into Mitch's eyes. "I worked with the CIA…I'm sorry…I'm…I'm losing my memory."

He suddenly rose from the table, grabbed his publications, hurrying away and out the door, pausing as if not sure where to go, then moving south toward Houston Street.

Mitch sat still, thinking through what he had just heard, and Wilmer Bracken's strange behavior. He decided he had to let it go. Just your average daily weird experience in New York City. A city of weird humans in a nation of weird humans on a planet of weird humans. Humans who fear change. Humans dulled by TV and smartphones. Humans numbed to climate change and endless war. Wilmer Bracken may have been losing his memory. But he was in the minority if he had even developed one.

Mitch checked the time, gobbled the rest of his sandwich, grabbed his Coke and headed to work.

"Gentlemen! It's a beautiful day!" Mitch chanted, his regular salutation to the blazered guards behind the large entrance's centered security station, a long, chest-high fortification of tanned varnished wood. Its polished wall looked clean and unexciting. But Mitch knew that, on the other side of that bullet-proof desk stretched a plethora of monitors connected to security cameras on every floor of the refurbished nine-story Ninth Street building.

"Mitch, there's snow everywhere!" responded Turk Matthews, the stout centurion whose muscled chest, like that of most of his cohorts, begged to rip open his dress shirt and blazer, his near no-neck flexing and sending his striped necktie splitting and sailing across the vast entrance, its force shattering a massive plate-glass window. Mitch smiled, imagining one day it might just happen.

"I know there's snow piled up!" Mitch countered. "But it's still a beautiful day!"

Turk laughed. It was a routine Mitch and the guards had gone through most days – especially stormy ones -- since *Center Stage* and the other magazines and papers had moved downtown into the newly revitalized building five years earlier.

The move had occurred after all 40 trade publications had been purchased and merged into one city and a single location by the new owners. Die Verschmelzung, the ravenous German conglomerate, had decided to make its introduction to the U.S. a most visible entrance. And although it was leasing most of the Greenwich Village building, it appeared to be the sole possessor, having embedded a mammoth gold and black "DV" logo on the entrance's floor and erected a like image towering over the guards on the wall behind their station.

Mitch touched the corporate ID on his smartphone to the small computer window on the security counter, entered one of the six waiting elevators, and pressed 4.

His fourth-floor cubby hole was well-placed in the middle of like stations for the other editors. It allowed him to call out on deadline night, easily summoning whichever editor he needed to question about a story as Mitch reviewed it.

His phone awaited with 15 messages which he quickly reviewed. One was from William Masters, SAG-AFTRA's president. He had already seen Mitch's article online and wanted an explanation and correction for the profane misquote the computer had created.

Mitch called Masters' smartphone.

"Mitchell Morgan," Masters said in firm salutation. "The novelist who calls himself an editor."

Mitch and Masters had known each other throughout the decade Mitch had worked at *Center Stage*. Mitch had written a feature about him after the talented actor had won a Tony Award for best actor ten years earlier. That Broadway success had brought lucrative film offers, and Masters – the consummate artist and dedicated union member – had become both an international star as well as a respected power within SAG-AFTRA.

"Bill, I'm sorry as hell about that fuck-up. The computer evidently decided to be its own editor. We're getting it changed online as I speak."

"Thanks, Mitch. As you can imagine, I've already heard from the producers' lead negotiator about it. He was quite confused."

"I understand. SAG-AFTRA's strike won't be much fun starting in New York today. We've been assaulted with snow."

"I know. I'm not in LA. I'm here in Manhattan. We've had a positive emergency meeting of the union's executive board and some of our famous members. I wanted to personally invite you to a 3 pm press conference at the union headquarters today."

"Today?"

"Yeah. Like I said, it's happened fast. But we want to make an impression on the commercial producers and the public while we have the stars here together."

"I understand. Can you give me a pre-conference quote?"

"I just did. But let me add that I'm here in New York to personally attend these meetings with the producers following our opening the national strike. You need anything else?"

"Who are some of the stars you have on hand?"

"I need to save that for 3 pm. You understand."

"Sure. I'll see you at 3."

"Thanks, Mitch. Wish us luck."

"Bill, I'm an objective journalist."

Masters sniffed a laugh. "See you at 3."

Mitch began writing a brief update to put online. The union had called an afternoon press conference following an emergency board meeting. The confab would feature some star actors from the union, though the president wouldn't say specifically who. But Mitch went on to suppose it might be a couple of the big names with histories of showing strong union support. He placed the update in the appropriate news "bucket" online.

"Mitch, did you get in that freebie I asked you to for Sheila's Costumers?"

Abigail Schulberg, *Center Stage*'s editor-in-chief was standing at his cubby-hole entrance, still wearing her waist-length fur jacket, fashion blue jeans and leather boots to challenge the icy walks.

"Abie! You survived the blizzard!"

"Barely. Boy, you have the right idea, living down here close to our offices. Traffic uptown, including the subways, is snarling and growling. Did you get in the freebie for Sheila?"

One of the plights of being editor-in-chief: keeping the publisher and advertisers happy. Which includes regularly putting a one or two-paragraph filler about advertisers that will make them feel newsworthy.

"Yeah, I got Sheila in. Page 7 below the fold."

"Okay. Good. Thanks. Anything going on?"

He filled her in on the SAG-AFTRA press conference, then she headed back to her office.

Mitch slouched to the kitchen to grab a rare cup of caffeinated java. He normally stayed away from it, but he was exhausted, feeling need for a pseudo-perk-up to help carry him through to the afternoon press conference he hadn't been expecting.

Sitting back at his computer, he thought briefly about calling Rachel. Then said to hell with it. She's left. Ball's in her court. But he said a brief prayer for her, an effort to transpose his resentment and sadness from his ego to a higher power that got him sober and keeps him sober.

He began reviewing news stories on the Internet. When DV bought *Center Stage* et al, the conglomerate had dedicated all the publications to a heavy on-line presence. This included signing contracts with *The Associated Press* and *Reuters*, giving *Center Stage* constant incoming national and international news, including for arts and entertainment.

The contract allowed Mitch to pull news stories from the two syndicates and put them on *Center Stage*'s online news site. That meant filling a lot of "buckets" throughout the day, first checking with the other editors to see if they had already seen and filed the stories, or as a heads-up that he would take care of it.

Mitch took a sip of java, swirled it in his mouth for full taste, and held it there a second. He suddenly flashed back to his morning at McDonald's. To what was his name? The printed mail address on that newspaper neoned in his mind.

He found himself typing it out on his monitor:

Wilmer Bracken

332 E. Houston St., Apt. 412

New York, NY 10002

The fact that he remembered that info clearly told him something was going on in his curious journalist's brain.

He then went to Google and typed in the search area:

"Wilmer Bracken CIA"

All kinds of CIA info popped up, but nothing about Bracken. Mitch thought about two of the publications Bracken had with him. Then typed in

"Wilmer Bracken CIA security spy"

The thing about search engines: they don't realize their own power. It takes your brief info and connects to some of the most logical stories, and sometimes the most illogical name associations. And on rare occasions mines so deeply it discovers extremely rare jewels without knowing it.

Mitch normally would scan three pages of references – some 60 links -- finding info he needed, or giving up. He found nothing about Wilmer Bracken in the first three pages. But, call it the Muse or maybe just stubbornness, he almost without deciding, kept looking. Then, on page 6, halfway down, this headline and subhead:

PDF: TOP SECRET REPORT: OPERATION GHOST EAGLE

Liberty, Sentry, Warrior, Viewer, Scion, Wilmer Bracken

Mitch blinked. Felt blood warm throughout his body. Before he knew it, he had clicked on the link.

<u>TOP SECRET</u>

CIA Infiltration of Foreign Nuclear Weapons Systems

For Eyes Only:

Liberty

Sentry

Warrior

Viewer

Scion

Report prepared by Wilmer Bracken, Special Officer in Charge

September 25, 2029

Executive Summary 46 pp

By reflex, Mitch suddenly looked around to see if anyone was watching. No one.

"How the fuck did this get online," he whispered to himself as he began scanning the document. Then he stopped a few pages through. Sent his cursor to top right on his computer to the star reading "Add this page to favorites". He clicked to have the link filed on his computer.

Then he sent the cursor to the PRINT icon and clicked it. He opened another general window on his computer so the document was no longer visible on his monitor.

He rose and hustled to the room with the copy machine. It was running off the document. He looked around. No one watching. As each page printed out he immediately collected it, stacking and holding the growing document close to his chest so no one could see.

Suddenly the copier stopped. It needed more paper.

"Fuck," he breathed. Grabbed more copy paper and refilled the machine. The copying continued.

"Hey, Mitch."

He quickly hit the pause button, pressed the printed copies tight to his chest, and looked around.

Mindy Watson, *Center Stage*'s Broadway theatre editor was at the copy room's door.

"Hey, Mindy."

"I just interviewed Natalie Siever who's starring in the new production of 'Anne Frank'. Can you edit it today so we can post it now, or should we hold it for next week's print?"

"Natalie Siever? What is she? Twelve years old?"

"She won the Oscar when she was twelve. She's fourteen now."

"And starring on Broadway."

"Yeah."

"What? Is she going to retire at eighteen and go to college?"

Mindy chuckled and said, "I don't know. I should have asked her when I interviewed her."

"When does it open?"

"Next week."

"Send it to me when you're finished. I'm heading to a 3 pm SAG-AFTRA press conference now. I'll try to look at it later today, or for sure in the morning. Then we can post it."

"SAG-AFTRA's on strike now, right?"

"As of today for the commercials contract."

"Okay. Thanks, Mitch."

Finally done copying, Mitch hustled the document back to his desk, grabbed a manila folder, marked it with the innocuous "Bracken", unlocked his desk's lower right private file drawer, stuck it in and locked again.

He sat, breathing heavily, now wondering just what the hell he was doing. He wasn't a Woodward or Bernstein. He was national news editor of an arts and entertainment publication, for Chrissakes.

He clicked back on the computer window with the Bracken document.

What the hell?

The page was blank. The document wasn't there.

He clicked back to the Google reference page.

The reference and link had disappeared, vanished from page 6.

Obviously some authority had discovered a top secret document that had accidentally, or intentionally, landed on the Internet. And they took care of business, digitally burning it.

But who? And how had it slipped into public view? Had Bracken done it? And if so, did he mean to?

Mitchell's head was swirling with questions. But he needed to step away from this. He had a press conference to prepare for, and current news stories to find and fill the "buckets".

Wilmer Bracken and his explosive document…Mitchell gave a gallows grin at the pun…would have to wait.

A CALL TO ACTION

SAG-AFTRA's New York headquarters on the fifth floor at 1900 Broadway bustled with activity of union members and media. Some 100 people were packed in the union's small auditorium.

Rick Sanders, SAG-AFTRA's longtime communications director, was waiting at the auditorium's entrance to meet Mitch and escort him down to a reserved front seat. Sanders logically valued TV media's presence, but he knew that the union's members, who would want detailed information on the conference, would turn to *Center Stage* for its coverage. It was THEIR paper, covering their industry, helping them earn a living.

Union president Masters huddled with a small circle of union leaders on the auditorium stage. Above them was a large TV screen stretching nearly the stage's length. It was displaying the vaster auditorium at SAG-AFTRA's national headquarters in Los Angeles, which was stuffed with stirring union members. Intermittently the visual would switch outside the headquarters where union members filled the LA sidewalks and blocked-off street, waving strike banners.

When the union leaders determined the TV news cameras and lights were settled in place, Masters moved to the stage's dais, front and center. He glanced over, giving a nod to Mitch, who nodded back.

"I want to welcome you all to SAG-AFTRA for this emergency meeting," Masters announced in that resonant stage voice. "Thank you for fighting the rugged winter day and joining us here. And thanks to our fellow actors you see on the screen there at our national headquarters in LA."

Actors in the audience and on the screen all began to applaud.

Masters paused and slowly panned over the crowd. Actors are good at dramatic pauses.

"No one...NO ONE...is more dedicated to a profession of ACTION...than the members of this union. We are ACTORS. Our mission is to bring life to every cinema screen, TV screen, computer screen and smartphone screen. We do this by taking a script and turning it into a living story...a personal experience for every viewer. Including YOU!"

He pointed out at the audience, mainly directly at the cameras in front of him as the actors in the audience and on screen broke into applause.

"Our dedication to this mission began with silent films, moved into talkies, and eventually into commercials, both for television and in movie houses, and for RADIO AND SMARTPHONES!

Again an eruption of applause.

"We are also dedicated to continue this mission by negotiating a new, FAIR, commercials contract.

Applause.

"But we have a problem. While we've come to the bargaining table, open and willing to negotiate...we've found the commercial producers have not been willing and open."

Grumbling in the audience.

"I have personally sat in on these early negotiations. It has become clear to me, and to our union negotiators, that we are not bargaining with producers across the table. We are being MANIPULATED...by an UNSEEN ENEMY!"

Shouts from the audience and on screen.

"I personally believe the commercial producers want to meet in good faith with us. But they are at the mercy of BIG MONEY! They are at the mercy of those CORPORATIONS who pay for their commercials. CORPORATIONS who don't care about US ACTORS...OR EVEN THE PRODUCERS! They care about only one thing...how much MONEY can they make...and how much

MONEY can they KEEP US FROM EARNING…MONEY TO MAKE A LIVING… SO THEY CAN POCKET IT!!!

The actors in the auditorium and on screen weren't acting now. Their shouts showed they were hungry and angry. Masters raised his arms for quiet. It took over a minute, but silence came.

"How should ACTORS respond to this MANIPULATION? By taking ACTION!"

Shouts and Applause.

"The 300,000-strong ACTORS of SAG-AFTRA have spoken. They have voted to STRIKE!"

Applause and shouts.

"Beginning today, actors throughout this nation…actors in every major city…actors everywhere there is a commercials contract…are now on the PICKET LINE!"

Applause. Stomping. Shouts and now strike posters waving wildly.

As silence eventually returned, Masters looked over the audience. Then came the coup de grace.

Masters introduced Bart Cummings and Milly Wadsworth, two powerhouse movie stars who immediately received a raucous standing ovation.

Cummings and Wadsworth noted how they both actually got their first breaks in commercials, and that visibility led to their stellar careers, now millionaires with their own independent film companies. They didn't mention that last part, though Mitch would in his article on the gathering.

But Cummings and Wadsworth did praise the actors for their courage to strike. Then they surprised all with this: Neither of the two would agree to a feature film contract or act in a new production until the commercials strike was settled.

That made the auditorium walls and their large portraits of great actors shake. It was an action that wasn't opposed to the union's feature-film contract. But it made clear that major actors might join them and stall the feature-film process. And that meant even BIGGER MONEY.

It also meant Mitch needed to get to his computer and file a story to get online ASAP. Rick Sanders, the consummate communications pro, was ahead of him.

"Mitch, come to my office. I've set up a computer for you so you can write and file your story."

"Rick, I owe you a lunch!"

"You've owed me lunches for a decade! Come on."

A steady night snow had renewed as Mitch neared his apartment, stopping first at the corner of Fourth Street and Sullivan for his regular peppermint tea. The lovely middle-aged Korean woman was about to close, but smiled when she saw him walk in.

"Grace, you can't possibly have any of that heavenly chicken soup left on this frigid night, can you?"

"I was just to put in refrigerator. Let me warm for you."

"You're a saint."

"You work today?"

"A very busy day. How was business for you?"

"Yes, busy day. Lots of coffee, tea, soup. Glad I have some left for you."

"How's your daughter?"

"She about to graduate from NYU. Then study for her master's."

"Good for her. Please tell her I said hello."

"I do that."

Mitch carried the soup and tea up to the apartment, deciding to take a hot shower before he ate.

Following the meal of soup and a croissant, he moved to his computer, sipping on the warm tea, prepping for his two hours of digest work.

Four years earlier, the seasoned journalist had begun to connect dots. While he enjoyed his work covering the arts and entertainment industry, his journalistic soul had deeper concerns: the planet, its continuum, and the geopolitics and policies that could destroy or save it.

He had determined that six major issues, six vital issues really, would be the driving forces for civilization's dissolution or salvation: (1) water, because it is key to daily survival for every living being; (2) nuclear weapons, because they are the major man-made threat to civilization; (3) energy, because it lights, warms, cools, and allows the world to operate; (4) technology, because it empowers the entire globe to connect in communication and education; (5) law, because it should prove the determining factor for whether humans are, indeed, civilized; and (6) surveillance versus freedom, because Orwell had made clear the dehumanization of society through surveillance in "1984". And the world was seeing surveillance today as a vast and still spreading cancer.

Mitch had dedicated two hours of most weekday evenings researching each of these issues, one issue each weeknight, deciding to logically combine technology and surveillance.

Then he had stumbled by chance, or Muse, onto a little online newspaper about health, with a masthead and articles, neat and clean and easily readable.

Study showed him that the paper was published through paper.li, a side company created by the Swiss Institute of Technology, who had developed amazing software garnering news stories, blogs, and videos on any subject in the world. It allowed a "publisher", curator really, to use the material, keep or toss out articles and videos, and also add other articles and videos Mitch might find.

He created a newspaper on each of the now five subjects he considered vital, and would spend two hours each weeknight forming the publication, and placing it on Facebook, LinkedIn, and Univerz, a new social media site which had become popular with high-school and college-age youth.

Usually Monday nights were meant for curating the nuclear arms digest, which he called *Global Nuclear Weapons*. But last Monday, the turmoil of the rising SAG-AFTRA strike had kept Mitch busy. So he decided to delay the digest until tonight.

Over the past two years, the nuclear-weapon nemesis was growing more and more serious. The Russian dictator who had followed the assassinated Vladimir Putin reportedly was secretly supplying nuclear weapons to Iran to protect itself from Israel, and to Kenya as a first move to unify African states for a move against the West. China continued to increase its nuclear arsenal. And in North Korea, where the ruthless Kim Jong-un and his daughter had disappeared, and his sister Kim Yo Jong had taken power, she reportedly was expanding the number of nuclear warheads while also increasing troops near the South Korean border.

Mitch would place these stories at the head of his digest, and add another 20 stories from publications around the globe.

He would also write a blog for the paper, explaining how this "new" Cold War actually had begun years earlier when President Barack Obama decided to initiate a 10-year, trillion-dollar refurbishing of America's nuclear arsenal. And how that led to both Russia and China beginning to increase their nuclear weapons. He headlined the column "Nukebuild: This will not end well".

Then, as with all the digests, he made a video, reading his blog column, and urging viewers to take actions of peace, not war. He put it in the digest, then placed the digest on Facebook, LinkedIn, and Univerz.

He thought about the top-secret document he had locked in his office desk. But he knew he would need to study it in detail, and check its validity before even considering writing about it.

All this gave Mitch increased incentive to pray as he rolled into bed and clicked off the light. His body, mind, and heart were missing Rachel. He prayed for her too, and, exhausted by a day of hammering cold and stressful activity, drifted into sleep.

FLASHING GREEN EYES

The SAG-AFTRA commercials strike was a month old now, with no headway and talks stalled. It was Tuesday, *Center Stage*'s deadline day, and it would be busy. SAG-AFTRA had called a press gathering, again at their New York headquarters. The guest speaker would be Casey O'Hara, the president of the national AFL-CIO labor union, the powerful parent organization to which SAG-AFTRA and other smaller national trade unions belonged. O'Hara was traveling from his national headquarters in Washington, DC specifically for the confab. And his presence should take the strike to a whole new level.

Mitch started the day breakfasting at the Broadway McDonald's just west of his apartment. He had frequented it over the last month, hoping to catch site again of Wilmer Bracken. But no go.

As he sat alone, munching on his Macbreakfast, reading *The New York Times*, a hand suddenly slipped two magazines on the other side of the table: a copy of *Geopolitical Insight* and also *Vogue*, the cover featuring a smiling fresh face with bright green eyes and shocking red hair in a gorgeous spring dress.

Mitch glanced up. His body jolted slightly. A young woman was sitting down across from him. A woman with shocking red hair, her bright green eyes looking at her tray of egg McMuffin and coffee. Her hair wasn't wavy and windy like on the magazine cover, but simply pulled back in a pony tail under her well-worn Atlanta Braves wool ball cap. But the red still flashed like neon to Mitch. Her face simply glowed.

How could he not speak to her?

"That's quite an ironic pair of publications you've gathered there," he quipped. Was that a dumb thing to say? Probably, but what the hell. It was at least a starter.

She gazed at him quizzically, her green eyes flashing.

"You don't think a woman can be fascinated by both fashion and geopolitics?"

"Yes, I do think she can be. In fact, I think she should be. I even praise it. I'm just not used to seeing someone brandishing those impressive titles together."

"Brandishing?"

"Okay, I overstated. It's rare for me to see someone connecting those two eclectic interests at one sitting."

She studied him, then smiled.

"So where do you usually sit?" She was ready to play the game.

"I usually sit at a computer, researching and writing."

"You're a writer?"

"A journalist."

"And who do you journal for?"

"*Center Stage*. It's a trade pub…"

"I know *Center Stage*. I'm a member of SAG-AFTRA."

Thank you, God.

"Well. Coincidentally I'll be covering their press conference today."

"With Casey O'Hara?"

"Yeah." She WAS up on the union activity.

"You're Mitchell Morgan?"

Shock.

"Uh…yeah."

He quickly slipped one of his business cards from his coat pocket and pushed it across the table to her. She picked it up and studied it briefly. Then smiled again.

"I've read you with interest since I joined SAG-AFTRA two years ago. You're a good journalist."

"Thank you." He tapped a finger on the Vogue cover, touching only her photo's shoulder. "You're obviously very good at what you do."

She grinned, gritting her teeth a bit, and surprisingly began blushing.

"I've been lucky," she almost whispered.

"Maybe some luck, yeah. But I know the industry. I know it can be a grind. Even a lash on the soul with its obsession with physical beauty."

Her eyes seemed to gaze through him. Tears even formed briefly, but she caught herself, moving back into quipping mode.

"I keep up a good face," she laughed with a slight nervousness.

"Well, you certainly have a good face," he grinned. "Tell me what really interests you about geopolitics."

"Ukraine, of course. And Russia's dangerous obsession with nuclear weapons."

"Bingo."

"What?"

"I curated my new digest last night on global nuclear weapons. I do it weekly to put online. Facebook. LinkedIn. Univerz for the younger crowd."

"How can I find it?"

"Well...we could become Facebook friends," he offered with an overexaggerated wink.

She laughed softly, studied him, but didn't bite. So he semi-retreated.

"Well, you can go on LinkedIn or Univerz if you want, put in my name, and you'll see the digest on my page."

"Sounds good."

"Hey?"

"Yeah?"

"What's your name?"

"Rebel Daley."

"Rebel? Really?"

"Really. My dad's a radical conservative from the South."

"But you're in a union. You're not a radical conservative."

"No…I rebelled."

They both laughed softly.

She was quiet, thoughtful. He decided to stay quiet too.

Then:

"You know I majored in journalism." She had decided to share now.

"Really, where?

"The University of Missouri."

"Good journalism school."

"Yes, really good. I had always wanted to work for a newspaper. Admired journalists' honesty and dedication…But I got sidetracked."

"What happened?

"One of my classmates, studying photojournalism, asked me to pose for a project of his. Shots featuring different locations on campus. One of the photos ended up on the cover of the school's alumni magazine. An alum who ran an ad agency in Kansas City saw it and contacted me."

"And the rest is history."

She let out a soft laugh. She studied him.

"I need to go," she said.

"Me too. Hey, how can I get in touch with you, I've enjoyed this."

"Me too." She watched him. "Look, I've got to go to Europe for two weeks."

"Work or pleasure?"

"Work. *Paris Vogue* no less." A soft, ironic laugh. "Anyway, I've got your card. When I get back I'll give you a call. Maybe we can have lunch."

She stood up, grabbing her magazines.

"Promise?" Mitch asked in a joking moan.

"Yes."

"Journalist's honest promise?" he said, smiling.

She smiled softly.

"Yes, journalist's honest promise. Bye."

"Bye."

He watched her go, smitten, knowing this is New York. And she's a globetrotter. She wouldn't call.

SAG-AFTRA's New York headquarters again was buzzing, its auditorium SRO as both actors and national AFL-CIO union members crunched in. Outside police had cordoned off a block of Broadway, the street and sidewalks also mobbed with boisterous union members and their signs. The same in LA, these images broadcast on the large screen above the stage in the auditorium.

Casey O'Hara cut an almost comic figure at the stage's dais. Short and pudgy, his red hair sprinkled heavily with grey, he looked like an aging leprechaun standing next to the handsome, taller, lanky William Masters, who introduced him. But when O'Hara took control of the dais, his blue eyes penetrated a now still audience, also clearly controlling them. The TV news lights beamed as he was being recorded by all the major networks and local TV and radio.

His introductory statement was brief: the national union has more than 16 million members, active and retired, dedicated to progressive, pro-labor policies. Always dedicated to an honest day's wage and benefits for an honest day's labor.

He then quickly turned that to SAG-AFTRA and the producers not being honest in their negotiations, repeating Masters' earlier contention that big corporate advertisers were controlling the negotiations from afar.

Then came his reason for being there:

"Today, I am announcing the AFL-CIO's new policy in support of SAG-AFTRA's courageous strikers. As of today, the AFL-CIO's over 16 million members will begin boycotting products sold by these major corporations controlling the commercials-pact negotiations."

He went on to specifically name those major suppliers of consumer products to every home and business, ranging from food and drink, to clothing, to cleaning products, and he included automobiles.

"We're talking about a $5 TRILLION market," O'Hara said in a low, determined voice. "When our over 16 million members stop buying those products, watch that money figure drop.

"And remember this, you corporations: Our 16 million members also have homes with families. And relatives who have homes and families who will support them. And neighbors who will sympathize with the cause we are so dedicated to here today."

Pause. Silence.

"Let's get started!"

Bedlam. The audience close to raging with excitement. The same in the streets in front of the LA and NY headquarters.

Mitch rose from his chair close to the stage, working his way through the throng to Rick Sanders' office where a computer awaited him. Beside it, Sanders had supplied a copy of O'Hara's speech. Public relations folks were at times devils, at times saints, and today Sanders was a holy presence.

Two weeks later the producers returned to the table, basically meeting all of SAG-AFTRA's demands, including paying actors a royalty for every time a commercial aired on TV, radio, including cable and streaming the Internet. The producers and union even agreed to form an active committee to create protective policies regarding the dangers of Artificial Intelligence, which in recent years had replaced them in ads with computer-generated images of humans.

Mitchell Morgan wrote about it all.

It was March now, with its winds whipping through Manhattan's streets, offering scents of coming spring. But the New York earth remained basically brown in March. Once on a bus, Mitch had heard a tourist complain about this. Mitch turned to him, smiled, and said, "You know that's what's amazing about New York. Everything's brown. Then they throw out the first baseball, and the world suddenly turns green."

That got an immediate laugh due to the city's fame for its baseball teams.

It was Monday morning, and Mitch was preparing for an interview with Linda Bowen, the brilliant actress who was now the new chair of the National Endowment for the Arts.

She had taken on a tough job. Congress, with a House controlled by Republicans and a Senate split down the middle, was stacked with radical conservatives in both parties who wanted to scrap funding for the arts, including the NEA and even ending PBS, the nation's public broadcasting system. Mitch would be asking her how she planned to handle that.

She was in New York to tour some of the Off-Broadway nonprofit theaters the NEA helped fund. They met privately at one of those, in the office of the theatre's producer.

Mitch started by telling her how much he respected her acting. He cited a specific film she had made about a nuclear attack on New York City. She played the wife and mother of a suburban family whose husband died in Manhattan, while she, her son and daughter tried to survive the nuclear fallout miles from the city.

"The film seemed so real," Mitch told her, "and your performance so moving, I actually have not been able to watch the film again."

"Me either," she responded, her brown eyes both deeply serious while with a hint of gratitude for what she later called his "tragic compliment".

That seemed to seal their relationship for the rest of the interview, which proved deep and honest. It would lead to later honest interviews as she negotiated the turbulent relationship with Congress.

Also, Monday meant Mitch would be spending a couple of hours in the evening putting together his nuclear weapons digest. He still had not seen Wilmer Bracken at breakfast or any other time in Greenwich Village.

He had read the alleged top-secret document on foreign nuclear-weapons systems prepared by Bracken for the president and his advisers. It seemed legitimate and thorough.

The 45-page executive summary report detailed weapons controlled by the nine major states: the U.S., Russia, the United Kingdom, France, China, Israel, India, Pakistan, and North Korea. The report noted that all African states were members of the Treaty on Nonproliferation of Nuclear Weapons, but that secretly Russia was supplying nukes to Kenya, while the U.S. was doing the same with South Africa.

The summary noted that the full study provided specifics including intricate designs, and maps showing pinpoint placements of all known weapons and some unknown even to allies.

Bracken's paper also listed efforts by the CIA to aid those states who were allies, and to sabotage enemy states. Those again included Belarus and its Soviet-supplied nukes.

What was in the report that particularly stunned Mitch: the U.S. Space Force was secretly arming satellites with nuclear weapons. It would allow the military to propel them back to planet Earth. Mitch's immediate thought was if drones can miss the mark with their missiles only miles away, how far could a nuke miss its mark if sent from space. Also, what would be the effect of one nuclear weapon's explosion on all the planet?

The study summary also opened Mitch's eyes to something completely new to him. A secret covert American program called Nitro Zeus, which appeared to be the ultimate plan for cyber warfare. Mitch had heard of Stuxnet, the malicious computer worm U.S. and Israeli intelligence agencies had developed and infiltrated into Iran's nuclear centrifuge program, and which had gotten out of hand, infecting computer programs globally. But Nitro Zeus was the ultimate in malicious cyber attacks: a program which would inhabit and destroy an opposing nation's entire infrastructure, from its military computer operations, to the country's power grid, financial system, and vital utilities including water. This clearly was a secret program the American public, and the world, should be made aware of. It meant billions of innocent citizens would suffer, and even die as a result of such an onslaught.

Mitch had become so impressed with the document's information, he decided he needed extra security for it. So he had made three more copies, stashed two at home, and put the third in a safety-deposit box at his local bank.

When he finished curating the nuclear-weapons digest that night, he followed custom, placing it on Facebook, LinkedIn and Univerz. He sat back, whispered a prayer for guidance.

Then he decided: Tomorrow he would continue breakfasting at McDonald's. If he did not see Wilmer Bracken by the end of the workweek, he would go to his apartment building and try to make contact.

THE MEMORY NOTEBOOK

All week, Bracken was a no-show at breakfast. So now it was Saturday morning. After his McDonald's meal, Mitch sallied the couple of blocks to the old church at Houston and Sullivan, trotted down the brief steps to the large basement auditorium for his regular Saturday recovery meeting.

He saw a sponsee seated among the faithful, and sat in the metal chair next to him. The start of the meeting was ten minutes away, which gave them time to catch up.

Had the sponsee started his Fourth Step yet?

He was just fixing to.

Mitch smiled. The young man had told him that last Saturday too.

"Might be good to revisit the Third Step. Get honest with the higher power, and see where it takes you," Mitch suggested.

The sponsee said he would.

"Mitch."

He looked up. Monica was standing next to his aisle seat, looking concerned.

"Have you heard from Rachel?" she asked.

"No. Not since her drunken call the night she left. I figured the ball was in her court, so I've never called her. How is she?"

"Not good. I can't find her. But I hear from other women that they see her on the street from time to time. She's into meth. Suddenly appears then disappears."

Mitch's whole body felt like a tourniquet. Tears began to form in both of their eyes.

"Hell, I'll call her."

"Her smartphone's disappeared too. No connection when I call," Monica said.

They stared at each other. Then the meeting started, and Monica went back to her seat.

"That's what this fucking disease will do," Mitch snapped in a whisper to his sponsee. "Take a beautiful woman, beautiful soul, and destroy her. Fuck! I hate this disease!"

His whisper had grown louder. He caught himself. Took a tissue from his jacket pocket and wiped his tears.

He looked at his sponsee who was watching him, an expression like a lost dog.

"I feel so…helpless," his sponsee whispered.

"We ARE helpless…powerless," Mitch breathed back to him. "That's what the First Step's about."

The sponsee nodded. They both turned to listen to the meeting's speaker sitting at a table on the auditorium's stage.

Wilmer Bracken's apartment building stood on the north side of Houston between Attorney and Ridge Streets. Mitch leaned against the apartment building's wall across the street, looking at the day's *New York Times* on his smartphone and sipping herbal green tea from a Styrofoam cup. He had his shoulder bag, meant as a carrying case for a laptop. But he usually carried just publications and documents in it. And today he carried a copy of Wilmer Bracken's nuclear weapons report.

He'd been there an hour, hoping to see Bracken appear. But he had not. Waiting had been easy in the air's soft chill with its hint of approaching spring. But he had been patient enough.

Mitch began walking, stopping and starting across Houston, avoiding the moving traffic. He leaned up against the wall close to the apartments' entrance, and continued to read.

Finally a tenant opened the door and hurried out onto the sidewalk. Mitch hustled and grabbed the closing door, entering the empty narrow lobby, trotting to the lone elevator, stepping in and pressing 4.

Mitch had searched Bracken's address online. Found a real-estate site showing he lived in a studio apartment with "condo quality finish and southern exposure". That meant, if he wasn't blocked by the building across Houston, he might have a view of the Williamsburg Bridge and bending East River…but he probably didn't.

Mitch stood in the hall, staring at the door to Apartment 412. To knock or not to knock…that was the question. He thought about how he could just walk away, go back to his peaceful pad on Sullivan Street, gather up copies of Bracken's report, toss them in the fireplace and offer them to the gods. Get back to his easy routine…easy compared to what might be in store if he went ahead and knocked.

He said a quick prayer for guidance. And wouldn't you know: the little voice said, "Mitchell, you are a journalist. A professional. And you're sober and meant to be of service."

He went ahead and knocked.

No answer.

He knocked again.

No answer.

Is three the charm?

He knocked again.

Silence. Then a voice.

"Who is it?"

It was Wilmer Bracken.

"Mr. Bracken, it's Mitchell Morgan, the national news editor at *Center Stage*. We met a couple of months ago over breakfast at McDonald's up on Broadway?"

"I don't remember that."

"Yessir, I understand. You told me you were retired from the C…the federal government, and were losing your memory."

Silence. Then:

"What do you want?"

I want to talk to you about a written report of yours I found online."

Silence.

"What's the report about?"

"I have a copy to show you, sir. I'd rather not speak specifically while I'm out here in the hallway."

Silence.

The door lock clicked. The door opened slightly, with Bracken peeking out, studying Mitch.

"I don't remember you."

"Yessir, I understand that you have memory problems."

Mitch reached into his shoulder bag and pulled out a copy of the report. He slipped it through the slight door opening. Bracken took and looked at it. Mitch could see he wore a grey sweatshirt and blue jeans, dirty white tennis shoes.

"Where did you get this?"

"I found it online. Can I just come in for a minute and speak to you about it?"

Bracken kept the door at its crack, looking at him.

"Do you have some identification?"

Mitch slipped his wallet from his side pocket. In New York City, you never carry a wallet in your back pocket. Too easy for pickpockets with sharp stilettos.

35

He took out one of his business cards, handed it to Bracken, and showed him his press ID and state ID. Mitch had decided years earlier he would probably work in New York until he died. And having a car in the city, a rented parking space costs as much as a rented apartment, which he couldn't afford. With no car he couldn't be tested for driving. So he simply got a state ID instead of a driver's license. He quickly explained this to Bracken.

Finally the former intelligence agent seemed convinced. He opened the door, glanced quickly up and down the hall to make sure Mitch was alone. He smelled of cheap aftershave. He gave a quick nod and let him in.

Mitch stepped inside, looking at the frugally furnished studio: a plain brown three-seater couch against one wall, a small coffee table in front of it; a single bed against the other wall, both couch and bed balanced halfway from the front door and the dark curtained windows directly facing the door. Closer to the door a small Formica-top dining table with two cane-back wooden chairs and a Dell laptop facing one chair. Off to the right, a small sink, stove, and refrigerator, and a door to what appeared to be the bathroom.

The door clicked and locked. Then suddenly Mitch was shoved up against the wall, knocking breath from him. Bracken quickly padded him up and down for weapons or a possible wire. Then stepped back and studied Mitch.

"How did you find me?" Bracken snapped.

"When we sat talking at McDonald's, you had newspapers and a magazine with you. They had your mailing address stamped on them. I happened to see it there in front of me. Journalist's habit, you know."

"No. I don't know," Bracken mumbled. He looked confused, thinking. Then suddenly added softly, "Yes…I guess I do know."

He handed Mitch his IDs. He walked to his small dining table, pulled a chair out for Mitch, and sat down on the other side, closing the laptop, sliding it out of the way and putting the printed report on the table. Mitch joined him.

They watched each other in silence. Then Mitch spoke.

"Mr. Bracken, as a journalist, I need to know if this report is genuine."

Bracken picked it up and began reading it. Mitch waited. After about five minutes, Bracken looked at him, his face showing a mixture of pain and frustration.

"I don't remember writing this…I don't remember. But…I was looking at some of my old writing. And this sounds like me."

"It's a pretty straightforward report," Mitch responded. "Not much jargon except for the technical descriptions. Direct and clear in the actions you had to take throughout the report."

"Yeah…yeah…" Bracken thumbed through some more pages, wincing, trying to remember. Then a sudden realization:

"Oh…here…"

"What?"

"This sentence: 'The Israeli denial of possessing nuclear weapons has proved a conundrum for us for years.'…Conundrum…I noticed in my other writing I like to use that a lot."

"So you remember what you've been reading? That's a good sign, isn't it?"

"Well, I was reading it when you knocked on the door. So…and now I recall that my superiors hated my using that word. The CIA doesn't like conundrums."

He looked at Mitch and sniffed out an ironic soft laugh.

"So do I understand your memory comes back?"

Bracken rustled in his chair, gave out a small moan, "Awww, god, sometimes. In small flashes. Then it's gone. I use a notebook to write down what I feel I need to remember. Maybe an experience. Maybe a simple action I need to take."

Mitch watched him as he leaned forward frowning painfully, then straightened up, looking at Mitch with an almost cold stare.

"It's hell…you know…"

"Yes," Mitch responded softly. "The ancient Greeks honored Memory as a goddess. They understood it's…it's the key to…everything."

"Yes…it is."

"Mr. Bracken…if you don't mind me asking…you're still a young man. What's caused your memory loss?"

Bracken studied him, seeming at first unsure if he should answer, or maybe how to answer.

"I…I…They drugged me…yeah…they drugged me."

"Who? The CIA?"

"Yeah…the CIA…yeah…"

"You remember that?"

"No. But I wrote it down. I wrote about my experiencing gradual memory loss…then it growing…"

"Why would they do that if you worked for them?"

"Over this stuff," he raised the report up and shook it at Mitch. "They didn't want me to remember this. And more."

"What more?"

"I was becoming a danger. Starting to oppose their activity…and my activity…in the Middle East. And here."

"Here? In the United States?"

"Yes."

"But the CIA isn't involved in covert work in the U.S."

"Yes. We are. I…have been."

"And you remember this?"

"I was just reading it…before you came."

He studied Mitch with wide, strained eyes. Looked away thinking, then back.

"You're a journalist. I can trust you." He seemed to speak as if convincing himself.

"Yes," Mitch said flatly. "I came here hoping I could trust *you*. That you'd tell me if this report is genuine. That you really wrote it. And that it's the truth. It's my profession, Mr. Bracken. I've dedicated my life to finding out and writing the truth. It hasn't been about subjects as serious as this. But my reporting has affected people, their work, and their lives. The same principle. I'm dedicated to it."

Bracken studied him. Then seemed convinced. He got up and went into his bathroom and out of sight.

Mitch suddenly felt a growing fear. What was he getting himself into? He wanted to get up and leave. But he also wanted to stay, emboldened by his own honest words. He *was* a journalist. He was dedicated to truth. And he was sober. He could *be* truthful. He could care about and help others. He had proved that through the sober years. And now it appeared that dedication was about to meet its greatest test.

Mitch heard some metal rattling, then quiet, then rattling, then quiet.

Bracken returned holding a thick stack of typing paper. He sat down and slid it across to Mitch.

It was a manuscript. On the title page:

ETERNAL DAMNATION

America's Endless Wars, the CIA, and I

By Wilmer C. Bracken

Mitch opened the manuscript to the next page. A foreword:

I served my country through working with the CIA from age 25 to 55. I did so with a love for my country and my patriotic work. But gradually events led me to a conundrum: I realized my service was not to my country, but to a corrupt government and a lethal agency that was propelling our nation through an endless and winless quagmire. I began to oppose this within the agency, and suffered the consequences. This book details my experience and those consequences.

Mitch turned to the first chapter, reading its opening:

Let me begin at the end:

My last assignment for the Central Intelligence Agency was to murder an American citizen within the borders of the United States: a covert and illegal operation.

Mitch stopped there, then re-read that opening. He wasn't breathing. He forced himself to breathe in deeply, then let it out, silently repeating what was his constant mantra: *Breathe in faith and sober action, breathe out fear.*

He leaned back, gazing at the manuscript.

"I...don't know...what to say."

Silence, then Bracken:

"Yes. I understand." Silence. Then, "Will you take this? Read it? Hide it securely? Help me? I want the world to know."

Mitch looked at the manuscript, his mind racing about what it might contain. What effect it might have. His thoughts were blurring. He breathed out, trying to relax. He looked at Bracken, who was watching him, eyes pained, almost pleading.

"You want to publish this?" Mitch asked flatly.

Bracken watched him, looked away, seeming confused.

"Publish it," he whispered to himself, as if trying to understand the logic of it. Then he looked back at Mitch, his eyes appearing sad but sure.

"Yes."

"Is this your only copy?"

Bracken looked at him, thinking.

"I...I've got another..."

He rose suddenly, moving back into his bathroom. Again rattling of metal then silence.

He returned, sat and stared at Mitch.

"I...I've got another copy."

"Just one hard copy? You've got it stored on your computer, don't you? Also maybe on a flash drive?"

Bracken stared at him confused. His memory seemed to be fading. He shook his head, trying to remember. He abruptly turned, grabbed his laptop, opened it and began typing, glaring at the screen. He paused, read. Then looked up at Mitch.

"Yes. It's filed on the computer."

"How about a flash drive?"

Bracken watched him, seemed irritated trying to remember.

"I…I don't know," he growled softly.

"Okay…that's okay," Mitch said, wanting to calm him.

Mitch began tapping absently on the table top, thinking.

"Okay. I'll take this copy with me."

Mitch slipped it into his satchel. Grabbed the nuclear weapons report and stuffed it there too. He stood up, preparing to leave.

"I'll start reading your book today."

"We don't have much time," Bracken mumbled, looking out at nothing.

"What?"

Bracken winced, thinking.

"We don't have…much time. They'll…try to…stop you."

He seemed to be getting weaker and slumped over, his arms pressing on the table, bracing himself.

"The CIA?"

"Yes." Bracken looked up at him, his eyes weak, almost longing, so distant from his earlier cold stare and suspicion.

"Do you have a phone number?" Mitch asked.

Bracken frowned, thinking. He reached in his jeans pocket and pulled out a small notebook. He flipped through it, stopped at a page and read it.

"Yes. I have a phone. But...it's probably tapped."

He looked at Mitch as if in sudden realization.

"This apartment...is probably bugged."

"So they may be listening to us now?"

"Probably...I'm sorry...I forgot..."

"Great!" Mitch breathed out softly. He thought about what to do next. He moved to Bracken's side of the table, took the notebook from him, took a pen from his own shirt pocket, and began writing in the notebook:

"I'll try to read your book through tonight. This is Saturday. I'll come back by Sunday afternoon. 3 pm. Will that work for you?" He looked quickly at Bracken's phone number there on the page, whispering so he would remember it, and showed his note to Bracken.

Bracken read the note, thought, and nodded yes. Then he took Mitch's pen and wrote in the notebook, showing it to Mitch:

"Be careful. They'll probably be following you now."

Mitch read it.

"Fuck." He thought it, but didn't say it aloud.

THE METH MANSION

The sun was dodging in and out between the city's tall buildings as Mitch walked toward it and back to his Greenwich Village apartment. As he reached Houston Street, he paused, waiting for the traffic light to change.

He forced out a heavy breath. He needed a sober meeting. Now. Needed to hear honest sober voices. Needed that concrete conscious contact with his higher power through hearing those sober voices. He knew of a meeting on East 12th Street, and began walking there.

He moved through the tall building's door to the elevator and joined a handful going to the Seventh floor.

Some 30 people sat in grey metal folding chairs facing a small table where the chairperson and the meeting's speaker sat. The well-lighted room revealed soft blue walls with the regular hangings of Twelve Steps, Traditions, simple sober sayings, and photos of the global recovery group's founders. Windows facing the street below were partially open, allowing a brisk flow of air to fill the room.

Mitch was breathing easier now. This was home. He felt safe here. He had felt safe from the first time he had entered a meeting, though he was lost and terrified. But the atmosphere of that first room, the easy laughter before and after the meeting, and even during it, mixed with the meditative silences as people listened to the speaker share her story of what it was like in those days of hell, what happened, and what it was like now as she worked one day at a time to live sober. And those clear eyes and smiling faces who moved to him, shaking his hand, encouraging him to "keep coming back". And he came back, and was still coming back 20 years later. This was home.

During the meeting he recognized a fellow he knew who had struggled with crystal meth as well as alcohol. He was sober a few

43

years now. Mitch thought of Rachel, and walked up to his fellow after the meeting.

"A woman I've lived with is out now. On crystal meth, I hear. On the streets."

"I'm sorry," the young man said sincerely.

"Is there a place you'd go…a place they gather for crystal meth?"

"There's an abandoned building south of here on River Street," he responded. "The building was gutted for remodeling, but the developer evidently went broke, stopped all reconstruction. So it's pretty much a shell, ripped up rooms with a roof. A place to get out of the rain or snow. She might be there on and off."

"I guess I should go see."

"You want me to go with you?"

Mitch watched him. The fellow meant it, but he shuffled some, as if uncomfortable.

"Maybe not, if you think it might trigger you."

"Yeah…it might…thank you."

Mitch turned to go.

"Hey," the fellow called gently. "Watch yourself. Folks on meth can be unpredictable."

Mitch nodded gratefully and headed out.

Before he moved south, Mitch walked to a copy center on Broadway. He needed to copy Wilmer Bracken's thick manuscript. Two copies in fact, one for the safe deposit box. He then hurried to his apartment, leaving them for safe keeping. Then he moved south to see if he could find Rachel.

The sun was an hour from setting as Mitch stood on the ditch-filled old River Street, staring at the dilapidated two-story red-bricked building. It looked like a former mansion. The wire fence around it had been ripped away in places, and Mitch stepped through one of those, walking up the half-surviving sidewalk to the grey concrete portal with no door. The building's dirty brick exterior was covered with vandalizing art of bright colors, and even a couple of peace symbols. But the inside seemed dark, almost pitch black.

Mitch stepped inside and stood still, trying to adjust his eyes. Silence. Hints of light now leaked through the boarded windows.

Then sudden movement coming from a room off to the left. His eyes adjusting more to the dark, Mitch moved to the room's doorway and stopped, looking in. A lone figure, a man with ratted hair and dirty clothes was on his haunches, shaking. He wasn't looking at Mitch, but seemed lost, suffering.

Then movement in another room off to Mitch's right. He stepped there, looking in. Two figures kneeling in a far corner, their backs to Mitch, their hands engaged in pulling a "flute" from each other and smoking it.

Mitch looked left and saw another doorway, a room dimly lighted. He stepped into it. There in the corner was a woman laid out, her back against the wall. She was unconscious, dirty, in a ripped dark shirt and torn jeans and wearing only one running shoe. Mitch moved quickly to her. Her face was grimy, her hair greased and unwashed. It was Rachel. A spent meth pipe lay at her side.

Mitch bent down, checking her arm for a pulse. He could see now she was barely breathing. She let out a brief moan.

Mitch stood straight, he was starting to cry, trying to figure out how to help her.

Then, suddenly, two hands grabbed him, turned him, and shoved him against the wall. A gaunt, shirtless man was pressing his left hand into Mitch's chest, his right hand holding a butcher knife. His eyes glared at Mitch, his near toothless mouth hissing out curses.

He quickly raised the knife, preparing to drive it into Mitch when…just as suddenly…he grunted and was lying at Mitch's feet.

Mitch was leaning against the wall in shock at the speed of it all. He stared down at his assailant, now heaped and moaning, half conscious. Then he noticed a figure standing before him.

It was Wilmer Bracken. He was looking coldly at the slumped figure at his feet. Then his eyes turned up to match Mitch's eyes. His stare was clear at that moment, in that dim light seeming free of confusion, even comfortable with the situation.

"We need to go," Bracken said softly.

"What are…you doing here?" Mitch asked breathlessly.

"I followed you…to make sure you weren't being followed," Bracken responded flatly. He thought about what he just said and gave a breathy ironic laugh. Then repeated, "We need to go."

"I can't just…go," Mitch responded. He pointed down at Rachel. "She's my girl…used to be my girlfriend. I need to help her. Get her to a hospital."

The gaunt assailant moaned, attempting to rise. Bracken quickly kicked him in the side, hard and sure, causing him to collapse.

"Hey!" gasped Mitch in protest.

Bracken stared at him calmly. "We need to go," he said again. "Let's take her out of here."

Bracken helped Mitch raise Rachel off the floor. They began carrying her to the door, through the rooms and out of the building.

Outside, close to the curb, Bracken took Rachel from Mitch, sat on the ground and lay her on her back in front of him, her head raised in his lap.

Mitched watched him, then reached in his pocket and pulled out his smartphone. He dialed 911. He didn't notice, but Bracken was also pulling out his own smartphone, clicking on it.

"911. How can I help you?" A woman's calm voice.

"Hello, we need an ambulance," Mitch said. "We have an unconscious woman. She needs medical care immediately."

"Where are you, sir? Your address?"

"Address?" Mitch was stumped. "I don't know. We're somewhere on…"

"703 River Street," Bracken said abruptly.

Mitch looked at him. While Mitch was calling, Bracken had been looking up the address on his phone's locator.

46

Mitch gave the woman the address. He waited.

"Okay, sir. An ambulance from NYU Hospital is on its way."

"We'll be on the street ready for them. Thank you," Mitch said sincerely.

He looked at Bracken, sitting easy, holding Rachel, gazing at Mitch. He had seemed growing weaker back at his apartment. But now he was anything but.

"You okay?" asked Mitch.

Bracken nodded. "It's a good night," he said softly.

The NYU hospital's emergency room had been frantic with activity. The ambulance staff had wheeled Rachel into one of the care rooms and left her, Mitch, and Bracken there. The two men sat and waited, watching Rachel, who was now breathing heavily, moaning. Ten minutes passed with no sign of a doctor or nurse. That was enough. Mitch lurched from his chair and headed out to the emergency room's front desk.

The busy clerk seemed less than concerned about Rachel's state. Mitch was about to curse her to heaven. Then Bracken had placed a calming hand on his shoulder, and easily moved him to the side. He stood before the clerk and said something very softly to her. She had stared at him, nodded yes, and quickly called for a doctor who immediately appeared and went to Rachel's room.

Mitch saw that the doctors and nurses were now in full swing. So he and Bracken left. Standing outside the hospital, the night was really promising spring, the gradual traffic swooshing past.

"Mr. Bracken, I don't know how to thank you," Mitch said.

"No need," Bracken said, repeating, "It's a good night. We've probably saved her life."

Mitch watched him. "Yeah. Maybe. I hope so."

Bracken let out a very long breath, as if he was starting to weaken again.

"I need to go home. I'm calling a…a car."

"What? An Uber?"

"Yeah," Bracken said as if struggling to remember.

"You remember where you live? Maybe have it written in your book?"

"I have it written in ink on my forearm." He raised his left forearm to show Mitch. "We can take you home first."

"Helluva deal," Mitch said with a tired smile. "I may not get your book read tonight."

Bracken looked at him, then away as if trying to remember. "The book. Yeah. Well...read it soon. We don't..."

"I know," Mitch interrupted. "I know. We don't have much time."

Mitch didn't read the book. He got through the first few pages, but his mind was racing, thinking of Rachel, that sad, tragic setting of an abandoned mansion, and those abandoned lives, and of Wilmer Bracken's swing from struggling with memory loss and fatigue at his apartment to energy, strength, and seemingly comfortable involvement in that rapid violent atmosphere. It was as if his moving from isolation and back into the world had revitalized him. Then, when the activity had stopped, he felt the deep fatigue quickly return. And Mitch could see him beginning to struggle again with memory.

All this was churning through Mitch's mind as he turned out the light and lay in bed in the dark. He began praying in an effort to slow it all down.

"Please grant us your calming, healing sleep," he asked. Two decades into sobriety, he now always said "we" rather than "I" when praying, understanding that he didn't get sober alone and wasn't living sober alone. He had a fellowship in sobriety, and a higher power overseeing them and all, everywhere. As he deep breathed, softly repeating his prayer, and praying for Rachel, for Wilmer Bracken, for all his fellows, for the world...gradually sleep came.

ETERNAL DAMNATION

Following a regular early Sunday meeting and breakfast with his sponsee, Mitch spent the rest of the day reading Bracken's manuscript.

ETERNAL DAMNATION – America's Endless Wars, the CIA, and I

Mitch was intrigued by the title, giving him a new insight into Bracken. America for decades had been engaging in ongoing or endless war around the world. But Bracken's use of ETERNAL DAMNATION, in Mitch's mind, and he believed in most Americans' minds, would engrain a spiritual significance. One aligned with the religious right and their City on a Hill image of the United States – what the political neocons see as America's God-given right to global rule. Exceptionalism. Bracken's title was actually challenging the neocons at their own deadly spiritual game.

Then the first chapter alone led him to pause in his reading, remembering to breathe. Bracken detailed his murdering of an American citizen within the United States: Rebecca Sadler, an academic at Rice University in Houston, Texas.

I was told that Sadler had been discovered spying on our secret program developing nuclear weapons for use by our Space Force. That made sense, since Rice University has had long ties with NASA.

She lived alone in a small house in a middle-class suburb of Houston. My orders were to enter her home when she was alone, kill her, and make sure all her records, including any research and computers, were destroyed. The best way would be by setting fire to the home and assure it completely burned, including her body and belongings in it. Then break into her office at the University and remove any files even hinting at nuclear weapons or even NASA research.

I followed those orders at her home. But because of my long experience in the Agency, and my beginning to seriously question our overall mission, I decided to search her study, take her lone laptop with me. As her house burned to the ground, I drove back to my motel and quickly and easily broke into her laptop information. I scanned the data at length, looking for anything indicating she was spying on nuclear weapons.

But there was nothing. She wasn't a spy. Instead, I discovered this, leading to my conundrum:

She was a history professor, and her files and writing made clear she was working on a highly detailed exposé.

She was writing a book connecting Halliburton Company -- now an American multinational corporation with dual headquarters in Houston and Dubai, and one of the world's largest oil service companies -- with endless war. And her research and revelations went even deeper and were of historic impact.

Bracken wrote how she was intricately tracing Halliburton's growth and connections with the CIA, and the Agency's involvement with the assassinations of John F. Kennedy, his brother Robert, and Martin Luther King. She covered Halliburton's intimate connections with the presidential elections of George H.W. Bush and George W. Bush, along with the CIA's involvements with the invasions of Vietnam, Afghanistan, Iraq, and plans to invade other countries as outlined in a memo from Paul Wolfowitz, a high-ranking member of both Bushes' administrations.

Her research showed that through decades of presidential administrations after Kennedy – no matter the various issues ranging from economic chaos to climate change – each president stayed the course on two main missions: (1) assure the U.S. directly or indirectly controlled access to world oil and rare minerals, (2) support continuum of the Military-Industrial complex with invasion of foreign lands and increased weapons production and global sales.

The plan carried on through Obama, Trump, Biden and Trump again. And now these few years later was continuing with the new president and Congress (1) supporting the oil companies' expansion

50

of oil production despite climate change, and (2) endlessly supplying weapons to ongoing and growing regional conflicts while continuing a military presence worldwide.

Bracken said Sadler essentially was outlining a decades-long secret plan allowing America to continue its endless global war. Or as he aptly titled it: ETERNAL DAMNATION.

"Nobody's going to believe this," Mitch breathed softly. Yet somebody must have believed it. Why else would the CIA order Bracken to murder this little-known history professor?

Then Mitch sniffed an ironic laugh as he began the next chapter. Bracken was agreeing with him in his chapter opening:

At first, I didn't believe such a plan could exist. I had never bought in to the various conspiracy theories. But I did believe in solid historical research, and finally the need to connect the dots of how my country's government kept intentionally striding into military conflicts, and how my agency constantly kept creeping into foreign countries to lay the groundwork for them.

*And here I saw the proof. Its effect on me was deep and dramatic, for reasons and actions I'll explain later. For now, I'll say it ripped my allegiance from the Agency. It made this one truth very clear: **I had spent my life killing the wrong people.***

So after quickly reading my American murder victim's material, I decided two things:

First, I would not break into her university office. I would tell the Agency it was too well protected by night watchmen and security technology, as one would expect with a university with close federal-government connections.

Second, I spent the next week doing my own research in the CIA archives. I began to see how the facts I learned through my own CIA experience were aligning with those revealed in CIA classified memos and reports.

I had originally received access to the CIA archives to research material for my own confidential reports. But as I began to discover the depth and richness of the Agency's archived material, I quickly gained insight into the CIA's and our government's secret global involvements.

"Okay, Wilmer," Mitch mumbled to himself. "You've got me now. Where do we go from here?"

Bracken then went through three chapters, quoting from CIA memos, letters, and studies, tracing the interweavings of struggles for natural resources – primarily oil, then moving into rare minerals – and aggressive activities by the CIA, the military, the international banks, the weapons manufacturers, and manipulation of the major media that supports aggressive war, though they call it defending democracy.

He wrote:

The ETERNAL War effort – the ETERNAL DAMNATION -- actually began as early as the Spanish-American War over Cuba. The US pre-CIA intelligence officers secretly planted a bomb sinking the U.S.S. Maine in Havana Harbor, catalyst for the U.S. invasion. An action vociferously publicized by William Randolph Hearst's newspapers in the U.S. as Spanish aggression, moving public opinion to favor invasion of Cuba.

John D. Rockefeller's National City Bank loaned the US government $200 million for the war, the money paid back by a telephone use tax on the public. (You must remember this was in 1898, before the U.S. had a federal income tax allowing it to annually procure billions from citizens for the Treasury.) After US victory in Cuba, including Teddy Roosevelt's Rough Rider charge, National City Bank branches began springing up around Cuba, hardly a coincidence.

"The war was really over the possession and price of sugar," Bracken continued. "Now American wars in the 21st Century are always connected to some country's natural resources, no matter how the government publicly plays it.

"Also, the Spanish-American War was the morphing of American defense policy from self-defense to invasive offense: invading foreign countries to take possession of foreign assets. And for funding the continuum of what would become the Military-Industrial complex: The formula for building empire."

Bracken cited a 1969 study by a CIA researcher named David Ravner for the background on the Spanish-American War, and also Ravner's insight into how it set the precedent for the U.S. approach to aggressive war -- a process which Ravner noted "was the basis for our trying and convicting Nazis over their aggression in World War II."

Bracken went on in another chapter briefly outlining the history of bank creation and involvement in war, beginning with the Rothschilds in Europe, then their moving to the U.S. to join the growing banking behemoths owned by Rockefeller, J.P. Morgan, and others.

In another chapter, he briefly traced the history of oil. But he spent most of the chapter detailing the Bush family, oil, and Halliburton, the assassination of President John F. Kennedy, and the CIA: much of this information he had garnered from the murdered Rebecca Sadler's research.

He began with Prescott Bush and Neil Mallon. The two had met as students at Yale. Prescott Bush would go on to become a Wall Street banker, U.S. Senator, and father and grandfather of two American Presidents. Mallon would move his oil-related Dresser Industries to Dallas, and would become head of Halliburton when it purchased Dresser.

Prescott Bush would write a letter noting that Mallon was "well known to Allen Dulles, and has tried to be helpful to him in the CIA, especially in the procurement of individuals to serve in that important agency." Dulles was director of the CIA, later fired by President Kennedy when he went over Kennedy's head by ordering the failed Bay of Pigs invasion in Cuba.

Bracken wrote:

Sadler's research, along with letters, memos, and reports I read in the CIA archives proved to me the CIA's involvement in Kennedy's assassination.

Following his firing of Allen Dulles, Kennedy made known he wanted his administration to take three major actions, which would prove a massive threat to the Military-Industrial Complex: First, to decompartmentalize the CIA, dissolving its great power; second, to move America away from war and nuclear weapons as specified in his speech to the United Nations; and third, specifically get American troops out of Vietnam by 1965, which he had so-ordered in writing. I believe this threat to the CIA, the Pentagon, and America's major oil and weapons industries led to the president's assassination in Dallas in November 1963.

After Kennedy's assassination, former Texas Sen. Lyndon Johnson, Kennedy's Vice President, was immediately sworn in as President. Almost immediately, Texas-based Halliburton's companies began receiving multi-million-dollar federal contracts. These increased rapidly as Johnson illegally and vastly expanded the Vietnam War Kennedy wanted to avoid.

Bracken wrote that, before all this, future U.S. President George Herbert Walker Bush – Prescott Bush's son -- had gone to work for Mallon immediately after graduating from Yale. Later, with Mallon's support, the younger Bush and John Overbey launched the Bush-Overbey Oil Development Company in 1951. The Mallon-Bush oil and political relationship continued to flourish. And the younger Bush's oil and political connections kept him close to government, including serving as director of the CIA before he became Vice-President under Ronald Reagan, and later President.

When G.H.W. Bush took the presidency in 1989, former Republican Congressman Dick Cheney became his Secretary of Defense. After leaving government, Cheney became chairman of Halliburton, where he stayed until becoming George W. Bush's vice-presidential candidate in 2000. With Vice-President Cheney as catalyst, Halliburton spent the next decade making billions of dollars contracting with the U.S. in their Middle East military invasions.

Wilmer Bracken entered the CIA the year before Bush and Cheney took control in Washington. By the time G.W. Bush moved into the White House in January 2001, Bracken – who had proved himself to be highly intelligent and quickly adaptable -- had been adeptly trained in vast aspects of covert operations.

Following the Sept. 11, 2001 attacks on the U.S. by a group of Saudi al-Qaeda-aligned terrorists, Bracken had been assigned with the CIA operatives who were "first on the ground" in Afghanistan within two weeks after 9/11.

The CIA had developed relationships with the Afghan Northern Alliance over the previous two decades prior to 9/11, so was able to quickly adapt to setting up America's military invasion. Bracken's first year of training, in fact, had included learning the language and history of the area.

"Our mission was to do whatever was necessary to bring about victory," Bracken wrote. "We integrated intelligence collection, communications, logistics, technology, and, of course, killed when necessary. In less than three months, we had overthrown the Taliban."

A year later, Bracken was in Yemen, coordinating a drone strike in the assassination of Salim Sinan al-Harethi, an al-Qaeda operative suspected of involvement in the October 2000 bombing of the USS Cole while it refueled in Yemen's Aden harbor.

Throughout the rest of the decade Bracken "toured the Middle East", involved in deadly assaults varying from solitary sniper actions to drone attacks, raids, and bombings of "Iraqi insurgent groups ranging from al-Qaeda to ex-Ba'athists to Shi'ites.

"The mission always was to do whatever was necessary. It never occurred to me at the time that these humans were citizens of a country we had invaded who might be considered patriots defending their homeland. To me, they were the enemy."

As he looked back on that decade, Bracken added he had often spoken to young members of the American military who told him, while having been trained in certain duties when in the U.S., they had been assigned to other activities in Iraq. Why? Because employees of Halliburton were performing those jobs.

A decade after 9/11, following his helping coordinate the drone assassination of Anwar al-Awlaki in Yemen in 2011, Bracken was assigned back to CIA headquarters in Washington, where he received a medal for his Middle East service.

But he was slowly starting to turn.

al-Awlaki was al-Qaida, yes. But he was a U.S. citizen. And the victims in our drone attacks also included his 16-year-old son, also an American citizen, killed two weeks after his father.

I kept thinking how I'd taken an oath to defend the Constitution of the United States against all enemies foreign or domestic. But al-Awlaki and his boy also had rights under that same Constitution. I had heard no one speak of that. Of even the possibility of capturing them, bringing them back to the U.S., and trying them in court. I didn't speak of that then. But it left me with a bitter taste, and my first real, deep feeling of guilt during my time with the Agency.

I thought about President Obama, who had approved the assassination. I had voted for him. He wasn't an oilman like the two Bushes and Cheney. He was a civil rights lawyer. And like me, he took an oath: '...to the best of my ability, preserve, protect and defend the Constitution of the United States.'

I heard him take it. And I was proud to be serving under him. But now I was asking, why didn't he consider nabbing al-Awlaki and his son and bringing them back for trial? Why didn't he order us to help protect their Constitutional rights? Why was the only option to blow them up? I left that mission and returned home feeling sick.

Then, through his second ten years with the Agency, Bracken was assigned to working with "economic hitmen", continuing efforts to engrain the U.S. in foreign countries, taking control of natural resources to benefit American corporations:

The economic hitmen were private U.S. citizens working for American consultants to major corporations, primarily involved in oil, natural gas, rare minerals, even fresh water.

The mission was three-fold. (1) The economic hitmen would contact the new president of a Central or South American country, and try to bribe him or her to let American corporations come in and plunder the natural resources. If he or she agreed, the ongoing bribe payments and plunder took place. (2) If the new leader refused, I would enter to see if the CIA could organize the country's military generals to overthrow the new leader in a coup. If that didn't work, I'd plan and execute an assassination. (3) If that didn't work, the American military would find a way to invade the country. Iraq was a perfect example: we had put Sadaam Hussein in power, then when he later quit playing ball, we invaded and had him executed.

Then, as he moved through the last ten years of his service, Bracken was assigned to coordinate covert intelligence and actions on foreign governments' nuclear-weapons operations. It was Bracken's executive summary on global nuclear weapons that Mitch had discovered online.

After filing my report on nuclear-weapons operations – and now clearly realizing our government was basically urging the planet's destruction -- my allegiance to the Agency had reached a point of near dissolution.

I believe my superiors began to sense this, as I was becoming openly critical within the Agency to our government's expanding nuclear policy.

I was nearing retirement age, only a couple of years away. My superiors encouraged me to take early retirement, calling me a good and faithful servant. I declined.

Then they decided to test my allegiance with a seemingly simple assignment: go to Houston and murder the academic Rebecca Sadler at Rice University. The woman the Agency had lied to me about, saying she had been discovered spying on our secret program developing nuclear weapons for use by our Space Force.

Feeling I needed to protect myself, I followed through on the assignment. But when I broke protocol and looked at my murder victim's research material, it completed my break with the Agency.

I clearly saw that, in murdering her, an innocent American citizen, I had committed the same traitorous act to our Constitution Obama and I had committed years earlier in murdering and not capturing al-Awlaki and his teenage son. For the first time in my long career, I actually grew physically sick. I literally vomited out my allegiance to the Agency and government. But not to my country.

Now the question was, could I silently and seamlessly separate myself. And how could I make amends to my country, the world, and to myself for my decades of murderous crimes.

I returned to Washington, filed my report on the Houston murder and arson.

*Next, during my week of researching the CIA files, I decided how I could make one last action and **kill the right people**.*

I saw that in nine months, the World Economic Forum would be meeting in Davos, Switzerland. The gathering would include the world's powerbrokers: the billionaire bankers and industrialists, the billionaire techsters, and the world's leading politicians and elected officials. They were the manipulators and profiteers of Endless War.

They would be in one location. The meeting area would be vast. But my training and experience in logistics and drone attacks would serve me well in this mass execution.

Then, unexpectedly, my superior called me in, said they were concerned that my recent months of work traveling and coordinating spying on nuclear weapons may have chemically endangered me. I was ordered to take a thorough physical examination, including being given shots to "test and protect me for radiation" or any foreign substances I may have been subject to. I did so reluctantly, yet I needed to play it safe, like a loyal officer.

I spent the next week, when able, plotting my attack on the World Economic Forum. I had nine months, but wanted to lay the groundwork.

Then, over a week after my physical exam, I began developing memory problems. I reported this to my superiors, who decided to give me early retirement (which they had already planned), honoring me with another medal and generous pension.

When I returned to my office to clean out my desk, it had already been done. And an armed guard escorted me for the last time from the building.

Now, I'm trying to put the last information into the memoir before memory leaves and I can no longer write. I've been to doctors for help, but nothing has stifled my growing memory loss.

I also need to figure out how to move forward with my mass execution plan. While I do this, I've no doubt the Agency is watching me.

This is where Bracken's manuscript ends.

THE BASIC FOOD

After reading Bracken's memoir, Mitch was deep breathing, praying to clear his racing mind. This led him to three conclusions: First, he must find a way to publish Bracken's memoir, and the nuclear report. Second, he must find out what Bracken did with the murdered academic Sadler's laptop and data. Third, could Bracken possibly be trying to complete his execution plan? Mitch didn't see how he could, with his obvious struggle with growing memory loss.

It also led Mitch to a deep question of faith: would the higher power protect him…them…in bringing all this to the public? And, in fact, should they?

His experience told him he couldn't answer that question right now. His experience told him to move forward with faith and sober action, whatever that should be at this moment.

His journalistic experience clicked in. He needed to go online, check and see if Bracken had actually killed Rebecca Sadler in Houston.

He sat at his PC, went to Google, and typed in Sadler's name, then "Rice University", then "Houston", then "death report".

He found an article in the *Houston Chronicle* with the headline "Rice Professor Dies in Home Fire". The report said the house was completely destroyed with Sadler's body inside. No mention of arson or violence to her body, which was beyond recognition except for her teeth. Firefighters attributed the cause to faulty wiring.

So there it was. Reality.

Mitch decided he needed to give his mind a break from Bracken. He knew it would be impossible for long, but it would help him to dive into two hours with one of his online digests: It was Sunday, and while he usually published digests during the week, he began forming a new *World Water Supply Digest*.

He stayed at his PC, opened one window and clicked on WQXR, New York's classical music radio station, and then another window, opening his water supply digest link.

The classical music and curating process were meditative for him, not as concentrated as the writing process he loved so much, nor as deep as meditation and prayer itself. But it was his way of being of sober love and service right now.

As usual, he quickly researched and reviewed articles, columns, and videos from news sites around the globe, choosing ones he deemed worthy, and placing them in his news digest.

Most of the news sites had been long established, ranging from *The Washington Post* and *New York Times* to *The Guardian* in London, *Le Monde* in Paris, *Tass* in Moscow, so he didn't need to read the articles or columns all the way through. The professional journalists and their editors had already done that. And they had followed the traditional newswriting formula: place the most important news first. He just needed to get the gist of each piece and decide if it would help readers better understand whatever the vital issue was. In this case, water.

He would also run into solid articles and columns from little known publications. He would read through to see if the work made sense. He wasn't concerned about political philosophy. A reader needed to experience differing viewpoints of reporting to truly get a world view.

As he had prepared the water digests over the past couple of years, he could see major issues unfolding, and they were growing more dire in the latest articles. Climate change was becoming more pronounced in its effect on the world water situation.

Glaciers were receding at a more rapid rate. Greater and greater seesaws were occurring globally with alternating major storms, floods, and expanded droughts. The droughts were leading to massive forest fires, dried up rivers and farmlands, and food shortages. And that lack of water supply led to corporations who bottled water to expand their markets into drought-torn countries.

One article showed that the bottled water market was booming: Global market size in 2022 had been $304 billion. Now, nearly a decade later, it had almost doubled to $600 billion as humans were finding it more and more difficult to access fresh water.

Meanwhile, all this was leading to more and more public protests, more authoritarian governments attempting to force ends to protests, and sometimes all this exploding to revolution in nations around the globe.

And, as if this wasn't enough evolving destruction, aggressive nations continued to invade smaller countries. Over the last couple of decades they more and more had concentrated their invasions on destroying water supplies, leading to massive starvation and spreading diseases like cholera.

There was some positive news, mainly in scientists who were finding ways to lessen water pollution, and even ways to capture water vapor, making it drinkable. But those were minor really compared to the overall evolving struggles over water, the basic food for human survival.

Mitch then summarized all this in his blog, then his spoken video of his blog, including them in the digest.

The situation saddened Mitch. But his job as a journalist, and a curator of these digests, was to try to give a reader a global overview of the reality. And he was continuing that effort this early Sunday evening.

He gave the digest's 25 articles and the blog one last scan for placement and importance. Then he linked it, as always, on Facebook, LinkedIn, and Univerz.

He checked the digital time on his computer: 6:45 pm. He had time to walk the couple of blocks to his 7 pm home group meeting at Houston and Sullivan streets. So he did.

The meeting brought ease to Mitch, with the speaker concentrating on the Third Step, reminding him of the top priority: conscious contact with the higher power, and turning one's will and life over to that loving higher power -- the key to being guided in sober living.

He stayed in his seat at meeting's end, thinking. The fellows rising and passing by, a couple saying hello, most moving past and outside.

Then someone was sitting next to him. It was Monica.

"Rachel called me," she said, her voice sounding both sad and relieved.

"Where is she?"

"She's at the hospital. She's pretty groggy. But she's alive. The nurse told her that two men had carried her in to the emergency room. She thinks one of them was you."

Mitch nodded.

"You saved her life, you know."

"They saved her life at the hospital. I just helped get her there. I'm glad I was able to find her."

"Who was with you?"

Mitch paused.

"Just a guy who was on the scene when I found her. He was good enough to help."

"He sure was."

Monica leaned back. They both sat quietly, gazing at the empty stage and speaker's table.

"She wants to call you. To thank you. But she's afraid."

Mitch didn't respond right away. He thought about the speaker earlier. About the Third Step. About the top priority.

"Monica, she needs to get well. She needs to get to meetings again, get a sponsor, and start on the Steps so she can get sober again. Top priority."

"Yeah. You're right. So don't call you?"

"Call her sponsor."

"Yeah. Okay."

Monica sighed, then rose slowly.

"Mitch...you did good."

Mitch sniffed a soft laugh.

"Thank you. Monica, she's blessed to have a good friend like you."

Monica smiled sadly, touched his shoulder, and left. For a couple of minutes, Mitch sat and watched the empty stage, thought about the top priority. Then he breathed out a brief prayer of thanks for sobriety, got up and left.

Monday, the day before deadline, was always busy. Mitch not only needed to check the wire services for important entertainment news stories and fill the buckets on the *Center Stage* website. He also had to read and edit stories from the paper's other editors covering the various areas of stage, film, and TV.

He also needed to write his weekly column. The week had proved so busy with personal activity, he hadn't even started or considered a column subject. But he got lucky.

Checking his messages, he heard the voice of the NEA chair.

"Mitch, this is Linda Bowen at the NEA. Could you call me please, ASAP. I have important news for your readers."

Mitch was surprised. The NEA had a solid communications staff that constantly fed him news. If she had decided to call herself, this would probably be worthy of a front-page story, and maybe even a column.

"Our problem with Congress has suddenly become an emergency." The talented actress's voice was intense, and she wasn't acting. "The Republican majority in the House is calling for a vote this week to eliminate our agency, the other cultural agencies, and PBS. They organized the effort over the weekend."

"Well, we know the president's yet another oligarch, and becoming more authoritarian," Mitch told her. "But she's a Democrat and somehow still supports the arts and PBS. Surely she'll veto any bill like that."

"We don't want it to get that far," Bowen said flatly. "We don't want to have to add that pressure to the other fires she's fighting. Bigger ones to her, like funding the military and trying to balance her stance on the climate change fight with her corporate supporters.

"We need to rally our artist groups nationwide. You and I know they read your trade paper religiously. I'm open to you now for an exclusive interview."

"Good deal," Mitch responded. "Give me the details of the bill they're proposing and where the NEA stands specifically."

Bowen did both, emailing him a copy of the bill and her public statement on the NEA's opposition, including their dedication to providing arts support for the cultural welfare of the nation. Then she took his questions and responded professionally and fluently. They were done in 15 minutes.

Mitch then banged out a quick article on the NEA's nationwide call for citizens to support the federal government's financial aid to all cultural institutions and the Public Broadcasting System's dedicated effort at educating the public. He placed it immediately on the *Center Stage* website, then messaged a copy to Connie Van Meador, who now laid out the weekly print edition. Make it the top story.

Mitch began writing a column based on his interview with Bowen. He would lead in with the current NEA plight, then expand to a view of Bowen's solid early tenure at the agency.

His phone rang.

"Mitchell Morgan."

The voice was soft and welcome.

"Mitchell, this is Rebel Daley."

He paused a second, surprised that she had called.

"Well, the globetrotter returns home! How are you?"

"Good, thank you. I know Mondays must be busy for you,

but I wanted to check in and follow through on having lunch sometime."

"You bet and you're right. Today and tomorrow are very busy deadlines. But things ease up Wednesday. Would Wednesday work for you?"

"Sure. But not McDonald's," she said jokingly.

They both laughed softly.

"Do you like pasta?" he asked.

"I love it, but don't eat it much. The figure, you know. But I can make this a special occasion!"

"Great! Do you know where Da Andrea's is?"

"You're speaking my language!" she piped lightly.

"Good. What time's good for you?"

"Is 1 o'clock too late?"

"Just right! See you at 1 Wednesday."

"Bye!"

So now, for a few minutes, all pressures had disappeared. The world was bright and every human was loveable. Mitch smiled, gave a brief silent thanks to the higher power and went to the corporate kitchen to make a peppermint tea.

Later, taking a lunch break, Mitch walked down Broadway, wanting to grab a tuna sub sandwich. As he hurried past McDonald's, he suddenly stopped. Wilmer Bracken was seated alone at a table near the window, eating a burger and reading a newspaper. Mitch went in.

He sat down across from Bracken, who looked up briefly, then back at his newspaper. He didn't seem to recognize Mitch.

"Wilmer."

Bracken looked up quickly, alert, intense and confused, seeming to try and recognize Mitch, who decided to help him.

"Mitchell Morgan," Mitch said softly to calm him. He handed Bracken a business card and pulled out his ID, showing it to him. "I'm helping you with your manuscript, your memoir."

Bracken stared at him, then reached in his windbreaker pocket and pulled out his notebook. He flipped through to his latest entries, read them, nodding yes to himself. Then he looked up at Mitch and nodded yes.

"I finished reading your manuscript. I'm on deadline at the newspaper. This is Monday. I'll come by your apartment Wednesday evening to talk. Will that work for you?"

Bracken watched him, trying to remember, then seemed calmer. He looked around the restaurant quickly, then out on the street, then back at Mitch.

"I'm sorry," he said. "I just didn't remember."

"I understand," Mitch said softly. "Will it be safe for us to talk there? You had said you thought your apartment was bugged."

Bracken winced, thinking. He flipped through his notebook.

"I swept the apartment. It's okay now."

"So, I can come by Wednesday night?"

"Okay. Wednesday night." Bracken pulled out a pen and wrote in his notebook. He quickly flipped through the two previous pages, reading them.

"I helped you with a woman."

"Yes. You did more than help. You saved my life. Then helped me save hers."

Bracken watched him, trying to remember. Then he gave a weak smile.

"It was a good night," he said, as if assuring himself.

"Yes," Mitch smiled. "It was."

He started to get up, then remembered their being at the hospital.

"Oh, there's something I've wanted to ask you. When we were at the emergency room, I was getting upset that they left her in a room alone, but weren't looking after her. I started to lay into the desk clerk. But you moved me aside and quietly spoke to her. What did you tell her?"

Bracken watched him blankly. He flicked open his notebook again, flipped a couple of pages, then looked at Mitch, breathing out in resignation.

"I don't remember."

Mitch studied him. How strange this was. He was sitting across from a truly intelligent and lethal human being. He had planned covert operations globally and killed globally. And now he sat almost helplessly across from Mitch, his memory fading more and more. Yet Mitch had briefly seen him exhibit his CIA skills when Mitch's life was threatened, muscle memory reacting immediately where mind's memory could not. Where would they go from here?

"Okay," Mitch said simply. "See you Wednesday."

Mitch reached out, and for the first time offered to shake Bracken's hand. The retired CIA agent cautiously reached and took Mitch's hand, then shook it, his grip tense and firm.

THE FOLLOWER

Mitch had spent Wednesday morning at the paper reviewing the new printed edition. Satisfied with that, he went online, reviewing wire entertainment stories, found a couple he wanted on the *Center Stage* website, and placed them in the appropriate "buckets".

At 12:30 pm, he left for D'Andrea's, where he had made lunch reservations for him and Rebel Daley. *Center Stage* executives and editors often took guests to D'Andrea's, so it had been easy for Mitch to reserve a table for two on the patio looking out on West 13th Street between Fifth and Sixth avenues.

Mitch arrived early for the 1 p.m. reservation and decided to stop outside the restaurant and wait on his date. He looked across the street and saw a man, probably in his 30s, wearing a Yankees ball cap, a light windbreaker, worn blue jeans and running shoes. He was walking past, looking in the shop and restaurant windows and away from D'Andrea's.

Mitch suddenly felt a cold queasiness. That morning, before going into work, he had quickly decided to turn around on Ninth Street and walk back toward Broadway to get some cash at the corner bank branch. The same man had been walking half a block behind Mitch and, when Mitch about-faced, he saw that the man had been watching him, but quickly looked away and kept walking forward and past Mitch.

But now seeing him again, Mitch's memory quickly dashed back to his first meeting with Wilmer Bracken, and what Bracken had said before Mitch left him in his studio apartment:

"Be careful. They'll probably be following you now."

Then he recalled the night Bracken had saved his life when the meth addict nearly stabbed him, and why Bracken said he was there:

"I followed you…to make sure you weren't being followed."

Mitch quickly grabbed his smartphone, raised it and snapped a photo of the mystery man passing by, getting a profile of his face.

Mitch's eyes trailed the man as he kept walking, turning left at Sixth Street and seeming to disappear. Mitch kept staring to see if he might reappear.

He wondered if Bracken could be right, or if he himself was becoming paranoid.

"Hi, Mitchell!"

Mitch turned, and the mystery man suddenly completely disappeared from ever existing. Rachel Daley stood there looking like the cover girl she was, her flaming hair shoulder-length, her electric emerald eyes sending volts through him. Her sky-blue spring dress partially blocked by a darker blue light jacket.

Mitch knew he must now be smiling like an excited grade schooler, but he couldn't help it.

"Heyyy!" His voice was soft and long. And he had to tell her. "I hate to sound trite, but, Rebel…you look like a Vogue cover."

She smiled shyly, then laughed.

"I'm glad to see you!" Her voice was happy, sincere.

"Me too! Let's go in!"

The hostess led them over the dark-wood floor past the tasteful walls alternating from old brick to classic wood mounted with butterscotch grain decorated with brown-framed modern Italian artwork. The rowed tables and chairs were of dark wood topped with white China and napkins, waiting erect water and wine glasses.

But Mitch didn't see any of that. He was walking behind Rebel, studying her graceful, easy model's walk.

The still glassed-in patio had tables and chairs of a lighter brown with small inviting candles aflame between the China settings.

Mitch's racing mind couldn't decide if he should offer Rebel the outer chair so she could face the windows and the world could revel in seeing her, or the inner chair to protect her from passing customers and waiters.

The hostess beat him to deciding. She moved and offered Rebel the inner chair, which she happily accepted.

Mitch found himself just sitting, smiling, silently gazing at her. She saw this and smiled.

"I'm glad we're doing this," she said softly.

"Me too. I'm so glad you called. Brightened a stressful day."

They both ordered pasta, she the homemade saffron fettucine with vegetables and olive puree; he the homemade ricotta cavatelli with shrimp and salmon in pesto sauce. She had a white wine; he an unsweetened iced tea with lime.

"So how was Europe?" he asked. "However it was, I'm glad you came back."

She laughed gently.

"Work was fast and pressured. Still photos for *Vogue* in Paris. A commercial shoot for Gucci in Rome. But I was able to stay after work. I made it to the Louvre and the Vatican."

"First time?"

"Yeah, to both. You ever been?"

"No. I seem to be anchored in the ol' U.S. Tell me what moved you."

Her eyes showed she appreciated his wording.

"Frankly both places were overwhelming. Just PILES of masterpieces. And packed with humans like Grand Central Station at rush hour. The day I was there, you would have had to fistfight to get sight of the Mona Lisa."

They both laughed lightly at her image.

"So you didn't get to see that mystic smile? I would think you would identify with her having to eternally hold that for all civilization."

She immediately got his meaning. Her eyes briefly teared, then cleared, and Mitch remembered that same reaction when they had first talked at McDonald's. She's a sensitive soul, he thought to himself. Be honest, but be gentle.

"I'll tell you what really moved me at the Louvre. 'Liberty Leading the People'."

"You mean the painting? Delacroix?"

"You know his work?"

"I know that one. But not because I'm any kind of scholar. I think I saw it in a music video or something."

She laughed out loud, then caught herself. She gazed at him.

"God, you are so refreshing," she said giving her head a brief shake, as if just being relieved of paying a light bill. Gazed again at him, then out past him, thinking.

"That painting has such energy. And it's such a dramatic statement of war's futility yet freedom's demand. Lady Liberty standing tall and resolute with the French flag, dead bodies all at her feet and ahead of her; live, passionate warriors by and behind her. And her relentlessly urging them on. And kneeling before her: a young woman or man – I'm not sure – in ragged blue clothes and a red-scarved head, gazing up at her in…I don't know…such awe."

She stopped there. She was starting to cry softly now. She grabbed her napkin and began wiping her eyes.

"I'm sorry," she said.

"No need to be sorry. Don't ever apologize for being honest about caring for humanity."

Had he really said that? But she looked at him, deeply, appreciative. And she smiled. He smiled too.

"I've got something to ask you," she said.

"Shoot."

"The digests you put online."

"Wow! You've looked at those? I rarely get any responses to them. I think sometimes about stopping."

"You had mentioned one when we met. I googled you. One came up, then another. I looked last night at the one on water. Those articles and videos paint a drastic picture."

"I'm both glad and sorry to hear that. Glad you're able to understand the reality from seeing them, sorry it has to be that way."

She watched him with a sad smile. He sat admiring it.

"I think Shakespeare right now would call for comic relief," Mitch said. "You want a funny dessert?"

She laughed.

"Not to be morbid," Rebel quipped, "but maybe Death by Chocolate Pie?"

"Don't' know if they have that. Maybe Dying Chocolate Mousse. Sorry not sorry."

They both laughed. He called the waiter over.

After dining, Mitch's paying the bill, and before leaving, she looked at him, her gaze a soft sincerity.

"You don't know how refreshing and valuable this time has been with you," she said. "I'm surrounded daily by big egos, including mine, I'll admit. Always on deadline and self-interested. But you have a world view, and a heartfelt concern for the world. I want that."

"I think you've shown you have that with your frankly eloquent description of Delacroix's painting," Mitch responded. "And I think you may have an overblown picture of my capability." He then smiled. "But if it's okay, can I use you as a reference on my resume?"

They both laughed. She reached over, touched his hand, then took it in hers. She gazed at him with those electric, emerald eyes.

"Thank you for this," she said softly.

"Back atcha," Mitch almost whispered.

They both smiled, watching each other like explorers discovering new lands, and grateful for what they've found. Then they rose and left.

They walked together slowly toward Fifth Avenue, heading east back to his work and her home, though Mitch wasn't sure where that was.

After a block, he stopped, turned quickly around to see if the mystery man might actually be following him, and now them. He saw no one.

"What's the matter?" Rebel asked.

Mitch thought for a second, then looked at her.

"Nothing. I think I just really want to remember this time with you."

"Well…we can do it again…can't we?" She was smiling quizzically.

"You bet we can," Mitch said.

They stopped at Fifth Avenue and Ninth Streets.

"I'm sadly leaving you here," Rebel said with a smile that did have a tinge of regret.

"Let's do this again soon," Mitch said.

"Okay. Let me check my schedule. I'll let you know in the next day or two after talking with my agent."

She stepped to him, kissing his cheek, and smiling. He returned both.

"Bye!"

And she was away in the soft spring breeze, moving toward Washington Square Park. Mitch was feeling warm and grateful, studying her easy walk until she faded into the pedestrian traffic. He began walking to work.

Then Mitch heard it. Voices shouting in the distance. In Washington Square Park. The journalist automatically began moving that way.

"Oh…shit!"

He suddenly remembered: He had received an email notice that morning about an afternoon rally to support the arts in the park. Obsessed with Rebel, he had forgotten about it.

He found a stirring crowd of protesters packed together with signs reading "Save the NEA!" "Congress: Fund the NEA" "Save PBS!!" "Freedom of Expression!!"

A scan and sectional count told Mitch the crowd must number about a thousand. Artists, writers, filmmakers, media creators were already actively responding to the news of the House preparing to vote on eliminating arts funding.

Mitch thought, so here we are again: In Greenwich Village, the soul of protest and resistance in America. He recalled photos and documentaries he had seen through the years: the Greenwich Village parade for women's suffrage in 1912. The Stonewall gay rights riots just down the road on Christopher Street in '69. Protests for women's rights and black rights in the '60s. And the continuum of vocal and marching opposition to what would become Endless War: World Wars I and II, Korea in the '50s, Vietnam in the '60s, Afghanistan, Iraq, Syria, and close to war now with China. And now this crowd defending their Constitutional rights to freedom of expression, of speech, and to protest.

Scanning the crowd, he recognized a few faces: Shannon O'Leary, the president of New York SAG/AFTRA, standing next to Joseph Cohen, president of Actors Equity Association; and members of the musicians' union who seem to honor every protest touching Constitutional freedoms.

And suddenly he saw Rebel. She had immediately moved to the crowd and worked her way to the front. She was raising a fist of resistance and joining the voices shouting, "Fund the NEA! Fund PBS!"

"Honoring your namesake," Mitch said softly. "Good for you."

He stayed for half an hour, listening to the speakers.

Clint Hoffmeyer, the highly respected novelist and activist, was serving as emcee. He urged the crowd to listen closely to the messages they were about to hear, and then to get active, contacting their elected Congressmembers and Senators to support arts funding.

Cyndi Kessinger, executive director of the Alliance of Resident Theatres/New York, reminded the crowd how nonprofit theatres rely on NEA grants as the catalyst to find other funding: "If a funder sees that the NEA supports a theatre, they know the theatre's a viable, dedicated group of artists, and become willing to also support their efforts."

Legendary opera tenor Phillip Ortega explained how NEA funding is vital support for opera and classical music venues ranging from the Metropolitan Opera in New York to smaller opera companies around the U.S. And how PBS was "the lone medium consistently through the decades bringing opera to the entire nation."

Congresswoman Sylvia Rossi, whose representation included lower Manhattan, including Greenwich Village, traced her faithful support of the NEA and arts in the city, state, and nation. She shouted, "This is the time for you to get organized and active! I'm not sure we can beat this conservative onslaught in the House. But the Senate is split and may not support defunding. Which means the bill will go into conference, and we may be able to save arts funding!"

The crowd bellowed in response to each speaker.

Mitch had taken notes, and now turned to go back to the office and write about it. At the crowd's edge, he stopped, raised his smartphone, and took a couple of photos of the vocal throng. As he began turning away, suddenly he saw the mystery man at the edge of the crowd, watching him. Mitch quickly raised his phone and took another photo of the man, who saw that Mitch recognized him. His stalker turned and hurried away.

Mitch shoved through some of the crowd, following him, but the guy cut around the corner of one of the NYU buildings. By the time Mitch turned that corner, he was gone.

NUCLEAR BACK PACKS

Following his 6 pm regular meeting at his home recovery group, Mitch headed down for his scheduled appointment with Wilmer Bracken. Outside the building, he buzzed Bracken's apartment. Mitch carried a bag with two cups of coffee.

"Who is it?" Bracken's voice was tense.

"Wilmer, it's Mitchell Morgan. I'm here for our scheduled meeting tonight."

Silence. Mitch figured Bracken was probably flipping through his notebook to remember Mitch and their agreement to meet. Then the door buzzed to allow Mitch to enter.

Bracken opened his apartment door and studied Mitch, breathed out restlessly, as if frustrated that he couldn't remember the journalist. He gazed suspiciously at the bag Mitch held.

"Wilmer, I brought some coffee."

Bracken nodded, opened the door and Mitch entered.

Bracken moved and sat at one end of his couch, so Mitch joined him, settling in at the other end. Bracken seemed to sit at semi-attention, somewhat relaxed, but ready to move quickly if necessary. Probably old habit. Mitch was tired from an active day, so he stretched out his legs and leaned forward, placing the bag on the small coffee table in front of them. He opened the bag and pulled out the two cups.

"I know you drank coffee when I saw you at McDonald's," Mitch said. "It's just plain coffee, no flavoring. I hope that's okay."

"Yes."

"There's sugar and cream if you want it."

Bracken nodded and took the coffee, opened the lid, and sipped it straight, slowly tasting the first sip, as if examining it to make sure it wasn't drugged or poisoned.

"I read your memoir," Mitch said. "It's damn amazing."

Bracken studied him, trying to remember.

"I was with the CIA," Bracken said flatly.

"Yes. Your manuscript covers your thirty years there. It's very detailed."

Bracken got up, went to his dining table, picked up his notebook and pen, bringing them back to the couch. He sat, opened the notebook, and began writing, evidently recording what Mitch was telling him to help him remember.

"Why did I give you my manuscript?"

"You said you wanted to have it published. You wanted the public to know."

Bracken was writing as Mitch talked. He stopped, looked at the writing, then up at Mitch. He was trying to remember.

"You say in your memoir you were dedicated to the CIA for years. Then you determined you had been lied to. That the agency wasn't working to help the country. It was working to help only the Military-Industrial complex and enrich the corporations who make and sell weapons. It's more complicated than that, but that's the basic reason."

Bracken watched Mitch. Then he dropped his head in resignation.

"I can't remember."

"Yes. I know. But when you could remember, you wrote your story. And it's a helluva story. One the public needs to read and learn about."

Bracken studied Mitch, saying nothing.

"Wilmer, you say in your memoir you had discovered that you were killing the wrong people. Those are your words: 'I realized I had been killing the wrong people.' Meaning the Muslims in the Middle East who opposed U.S. intervention."

Wilmer listened intently, thought, then shook his head in frustration.

"I need to read it again."

"Okay. But I have a question for you. You say in the manuscript that, to make amends to your country and yourself, you had decided to start killing the 'right people'. Your words: 'the right people'. You say you were planning to use your skills with logistics and drone killings to wipe out all the corporate, financial and political leaders at the next World Economic Forum in Switzerland. Next January."

Bracken watched him. He clearly didn't recall any of that.

"My question is this: Did you, in fact, put together an arsenal with drones and formulate a specific plan of attack? Your memoir doesn't mention that."

Bracken frowned, thinking.

"I don't know."

"I'm also wondering if you recruited anyone to help you."

Bracken was starting to get upset. He pounded on the arm of the couch in frustration.

"I don't know!"

"Okay. Okay," Mitch said in an effort to calm him. "But could you search your papers, your files you have anywhere, and see if you recorded any information about that?"

"I'll look. If I can remember, I'll look."

He took his notebook and wrote in it.

"Wilmer, I'm going to see if I can get somebody to publish your memoir. And your report on foreign nuclear weapons programs. It's classified. But, hell, everything the government writes these days is classified."

Bracken was writing as Mitch talked.

"I don't remember a report on nukes," he said.

"I understand," Mitch said sensitively.

Mitch took a big gulp of coffee and sat, thinking.

"Wilmer, I also want to know: Today, would you still be willing to follow through on your plans to…as you say…'kill the right people'?"

Bracken watched Mitch. His expression showed the question seemed foreign to him. He simply shook his head, indicating he didn't know.

Mitch nodded, rose to leave, then paused.

"Oh, Wilmer. When we first talked you said, now that I'd contacted you, the CIA might start following me."

Bracken watched him, not responding.

"I know. You don't remember that. But I sure remembered. And there is a guy that's been following me. I took his photo."

Mitch took out his smartphone, maneuvered to the two photos, showing each one to Bracken.

"These are too far away for me to tell…"

Mitch took the phone, adjusted the photos to closer views, and showed each to Bracken.

"I can't tell if I know him or not. I'd like to study these more."

"Give me your smartphone, and I'll transfer copies to you."

Bracken did, and Mitch did.

"While we're at it, I'm going to take a photo of myself with your phone, so you can check it any time you don't remember me. Okay?"

Bracken nodded approval.

"Hell, if I'm being followed, the CIA already knows what I look like. But this should help you."

Mitch took his own photo with Bracken's phone and gave the device to its owner. Bracken looked at the photo, then at Mitch.

"Thank you," he said.

"Okay," Mitch said. "I'll do some research, make a couple of calls to see about getting these documents published. Today is Wednesday. I'll be back in touch this weekend. I'll come by Saturday afternoon. Okay?"

Bracken was writing in his notebook. "Okay," he said.

Scanning the newswires at work Thursday, Mitch saw that artists, writers, filmmakers, media personalities around the nation were all answering the call to fight defunding of the federal cultural agencies and PBS. Reports showed that senators up for re-election, including Republicans, were starting to voice support for continued funding, and some Republican congressmembers, also feeling the pressure, were having a change of heart. Mitch wrote an article summarizing this and placed it on the *Center Stage* website.

As he was preparing to leave for the day, his phone rang.

"Mitchell, it's Rebel," the soft voice said.

"Go ahead," he rasped, trying to imitate Clint Eastwood. "Make my day. Tell me I didn't repel you at lunch."

She laughed softly.

"Hey, my agent said I'm free for another week before I have to fly out. How about you come over for dinner Saturday night?"

"At your place?"

"Yeah."

"I'd love to. Rebel, where *is* your place?"

"That would help, wouldn't it," she laughed. "I'm in Soho."

"Soho. Rebel. I don't have any clothes that are acceptable in Soho."

She laughed.

"Yeah, right. Rents are outrageous here. But you'll be fine. You'll be with me."

"That's perfect. Because if I'm with you, nobody will be looking at me."

"Plus nobody will see you in your pauper's wear at my place. I live alone."

"I'll be right over!"

They both laughed. Mitch was finding it easy to laugh with her.

"How about 6 o'clock Saturday evening? Is that too early?" she asked.

"Fits my schedule, tight as a gunfighter's leather glove."

"Okay, gunfighter. I'll see you at six. I'm looking forward to it!"

"Me too," he responded softly. "Thank you. See you Saturday."

"Bye."

So Rebel Daley lived in Soho with its ocean of artist's lofts with rising prices, trendy boutiques with rising prices, restaurants with rising prices...

Figures, thought Mitch. She's obviously a hot model now with a good agent demanding top money for her time and beauty. Good for her, Mitch thought. He hoped she was using that money well, because fashion popularity can be fleeting. He figured Rebel, bright and aware, knew that.

Saturday came too quickly to deal with Wilmer Bracken, but not quickly enough to see Rebel Daley. But before Mitch did either, he needed to make one of his many Saturday visits to his office. The newspaper might be closed on weekends, but the national news editor seemed to never catch up.

The House had barely voted on Thursday afternoon to defund cultural agencies and PBS. But the Senate late Friday had responded, voting to continue funding it all. So Congresswoman Sylvia Rossi had been right. The legislation would now go into a conference committee made up of select House members and Senators, and they would bang out a compromise which would allow funding. Mitch would need to write and post a story about that today.

"Danny! Danny! Ever alert and protecting the castle!"

Mitch was calling to the weekend security guard who maintained the desk in the main lobby. His powerful physique mirrored the guards who worked there during the week, but Danny was more at ease. He didn't have to deal with the constant traffic from weekday work.

"Mitch, where the hell you been, man? I ain't seen you since the last full moon!"

"Aww, you can't keep a lover like me in the office 24/7, Danny! In fact, I got a big date tonight!"

"You're kiddin' me."

"Journalist's truth!"

"Good for you. I hope you get laid."

"I don't get laid, Dan. I just make love."

"Uh oh! Guys with that attitude end up gettin' married!"

"Whoa! Thanks for telling me! I'll need to reroute my philosophy!"

They both laughed as Mitch swiped his security card across the counter's computer light.

"Hey, Danny. I only see you here on Saturdays. Do they pay you that much you only work one day a week?"

"Naw. This is just one of my security gigs. I work for a guy who keeps me busy."

"Who's that?"

"If I told ya, I'd have to kill ya," he winked. Then he paused, looked at Mitch, and smiled. He had something he wanted to share.

"This is in confidence, alright? Don't your ass write about this."

"Danny, I write about show business. Does it deal with show business?"

"Far from it."

The guard looked around, leaned across the counter to speak softly.

"I was in Washington last week with my boss. At a meeting with the feds. Security guys in a closed meeting."

"Maybe you'd better not tell me."

Danny didn't hear him.

"These fed security guys shared with us a big worry. They talked about these nukes…bombs y'know…nukes that fit in a back pack. And five of these nuke back packs were reported missing."

Mitch blinked and studied Danny.

"From Washington?" Mitch asked.

"Naw. From Moscow."

"They disappeared from Russia?"

"Yeah. They're fed security guys, y'know. They know about nukes all over the world. And they had all hands on deck working to make sure none of those back packs got into the U.S."

"Well, that's good to know, right? That they're on top if it?"

"You ain't shittin'. And they're on TOP of it!"

"Hearing you're in on stuff like that, I'm going to have to ask you to start taking good care of yourself, Danny. 'Cause I like you!"

"I had to tell you 'cause I know you're interested in that shit."

"How do you know that?"

"I read your online digest about nukes."

"No shit?"

"Yeah. That's good stuff. It helps keep me up to date. Then I talk to my boss, and he's impressed I know so much!"

"And that's exactly why I put that digest together every week, Dan. So you can shine!"

Danny laughed.

"But don't go putting it in that digest either, what I just told you. Okay?"

"My lips and my online digest are both sealed," Mitch said as he moved into the elevator and the doors closed.

Settling in at his desk, Mitch continued to reflect on his talk with Danny. He recalled that Wilmer Bracken's nuclear weapons report had included a brief description of the nuclear back packs. Mitch

84

hadn't thought much about it at the time, since the report was thick with information about nations' complete nuclear arsenals, and ways the CIA attempted to monitor, and in some cases, disrupt them.

But sitting there, thinking about only the nuclear back packs, and what devastation even one of them could cause…both its destructive explosion and the spreading radiation that would follow…made Mitch more sad than afraid.

"Humans…we're so crazy," he mumbled.

Then a sudden, truly fearful thought occurred to him: What if Wilmer Bracken had decided to make his revenge attack easier? What if, instead of a handful of drones as he had indicated, he had decided to use a nuclear weapon…perhaps a nuclear back pack…to wreak havoc on the World Economic Forum?

That might not matter, since Bracken was in no mental shape to follow through on such a plan anymore. And he hadn't written about even considering that in his memoir. But his memoir had ended suddenly, as if he had been interrupted. Or wasn't able to write clearly any more. Mitch was considering all this as he absently scrolled through news stories online.

He stopped, seeing he wasn't really getting anywhere. He would have to ask Bracken about nukes when he spoke to him later that day.

Then, as the heart will have it, Wilmer Bracken suddenly disappeared. Mitch needed to call Rebel.

"Hello."

"Rebel, it's Mitch. Mitchell Morgan."

She laughed. "Yes, Mitchell Morgan. I know who you are…You're not calling to cancel, are you? I'm making a great pasta!"

"No! I'm going to be there at six sharp…if…"

"If what?"

"If you'll give me the address. You told me you live in Soho, but we were enjoying each other so much, you forgot to tell me…and I forgot to ask…for your address."

"Ohhhh! Silly me. 307 West Broadway. Unit 6."

"Thank you!"

"Okay. I'll see you at 6! And on 6!"

"You're quick today, Ms. Daley!"

"You can call me The Cat. Bye!"

Mitch thought a moment. His journalist's habit kicked in. He googled 307 West Broadway.

"The building has stunning full-floor lofts located in the heart of elegant Soho," the website said. "Loft rents run from $17,500 to $20,000 a month…"

"Holy shit!" Mitch whispered. "If I lived there, my annual salary would be wiped out after a college semester!"

He leaned back, laughed, thinking to himself, "Mitchell Morgan, what are you getting into here?"

And then he thought, yeah. As if dealing with an amnesiac ex-CIA whistleblower-revenger isn't enough.

That led him to pray.

Wilmer Bracken cracked open the door, looked at Mitch, then at his smartphone, evidently at Mitch's photo, then opened the door, locking it behind his visitor.

They sat on the couch. Mitch had brought more coffee, and set the cups on the coffee table.

The afternoon light was starting to dim, and Bracken turned on the floor lamp next to the couch. He got up, went and closed the dark curtains on his windows. Then he returned, sat, and picked up his notebook and a pen from the coffee table. Then he set them down, taking the coffee, opening and sipping it as Mitch leaned back thinking.

"Wilmer, I've got a question about your memoir."

"I've been reading it again," Bracken said. "I can't really remember what I read. Unless I read and re-read some part. Then I can almost remember it for a day."

"Are you writing at all?"

"I can't. If I try, only three- or four-word sentences. That's all I can manage. I can talk, and make sense. But not when I write."

"Do you have speaker-write on your computer?"

"What?"

"Speaker-write. You can talk to your computer and it will write for you. That way you can see your writing as the computer types it. And you can make changes."

"I don't know."

Mitch got up and went to Bracken's laptop on the dining table.

"Okay if I open this?"

"Yes."

Mitch opened it, the screen lighted. Bracken's window was on a document where he had attempted to write. Mitch didn't read it. He looked at the top of the window and all the function designations.

"Yeah. You do have it. You want me to show you?"

Bracken picked up this notebook and pen and walked to the table. Mitch showed him the speaker-write designation. Bracken wrote in his notebook.

Mitch sat down, clicked on the designation. A flickering light came on the computer screen's cursor, indicating the function was on.

"Wilmer Bracken will start using speaker-write," Mitch said. The computer screen filled with text quoting Mitch. Mitch looked at Bracken who was watching the screen. He looked at Mitch, nodded yes, and wrote in his notebook.

"Let me try it," Bracken said. He sat at the screen, clicked the designation, saw the light, and spoke.

"I'm going to write."

The screen filled with the text. Bracken looked at Mitch and nodded yes.

"Thank you," he said.

"You're welcome."

Mitch walked back to the couch and sat. Bracken joined him, and both sipped on coffee.

"I want to ask you about something in your confidential nuclear weapons report."

"I don't remember a nuclear weapons report."

"I understand. You wrote briefly about nuclear weapons now in back packs."

Wilmer opened his notebook and began writing.

"I know you can't remember this, but please look and see if you put together any information about possibly using a nuclear back pack in attacking the World Economic Forum."

Bracken looked up at him. He let out a brief frustrated breath, then wrote more.

"I was going to attack the World Economic Forum," Bracken repeated, evidently writing it down.

Mitch wanted to know what he was writing. But he decided, if Bracken had trouble organizing his writing, he didn't want to embarrass him. He could simply remind him about information Mitch needed each time they talked.

This has to be hell for him, Mitch thought to himself.

"I'll look to see if I can find anything," Bracken said.

"I've also begun researching what to do about getting you published," Mitch told him. "The first thing I need to do is see what the legal consequences might be for you, and for me by helping you, if this memoir gets published. And what consequences for me if I publish the nuke report."

"What are you going to do?" Bracken asked.

Mitch looked around.

"You swept the place, you said. It's clear of bugs?"

"I swept it right before you came."

"Good."

They watched each other.

"I know a lawyer in Boston," Mitch said. "I'm going to take the train up there next weekend and meet with him. He knows about these things. His name…"

"Don't tell me his name," Bracken interrupted.

"Okay. Yeah. And I've a publisher friend I want to speak with. I'll report back to you on both of those."

"We may be running out of time," Bracken said.

"I know. But I'm doing the best I can while trying to keep my job."

"Yes."

Mitch got up and began moving toward the door.

"Gotta go. Believe it or not, I got a date."

Bracken sat and watched him.

"Oh, Wilmer. One other important thing. The guy I told you was following me. I gave you the two photos I took. I talked to you about that on Wednesday. But that's the last time I saw him. I haven't seen him at all the last three days. I guess that's a good sign?"

Bracken watched Mitch. Then he took his notebook and thumbed through his last few pages.

"You don't need to worry about him anymore," Bracken said simply.

"What do you mean?"

"He won't bother you anymore."

"Why not?"

"I took care of that."

"How did you take care of it?"

"I took care of it."

Bracken stared at Mitch with a strange, matter-of-fact expression. Not a glare. But a look of quiet determination. It was clear he wasn't going to say any more about it.

Not knowing what to say, Mitch nodded and left.

Mitch couldn't help but turn and look as he walked, feeling paranoid he might have another follower, if the mystery man was no longer around…whatever that meant.

He also began to question if he needed to continue doing this.

"You knew this was going to be dangerous," Mitch said to himself. "Any idiot would know this was going to be dangerous. And it can get more dangerous. Shit!"

As he walked to Rebel's, he continued to look around. And to pray. He didn't want to be followed. And he certainly didn't want anybody following him to where Rebel lived.

YOU CAN'T TAKE THAT AWAY FROM ME

The door opened. This must have been how Paris felt his first night with Helen of Troy, Mitch thought. He recalled the first time he had taken a swig of bourbon when he was 13 years old. He had later shared at a recovery meeting, "I felt like I had just kissed the sky."

This feeling, right now, was deeper, and higher.

Rebel Daley stood there in semi-shadow, her apartment's comfortable lighting behind her. She seemed, to Mitch, almost a dream. If you could get past that classic face, you could see she was dressed in sweet simplicity: a plain white blouse and baggy khaki pants with running shoes. But on her, the work of art would require an expensive frame.

"Well, if it isn't Mitchell Morgan! Defender of American culture!"

Mitch breathed in deeply and out to relax. He smiled, tried to think of a worthy comeback, but nothing came.

"Hi," he said, gazing at her.

She seemed to understand her effect on him. She studied him for a moment, then stepped to him, kissed his cheek, fixed her glowing eyes on his, and decided to break the spell.

"You're hungry, right?"

"What do you have in mind?" he joked softly.

She laughed, punched him on the arm, and pulled him inside, shutting the door.

"Plop yourself and relax on my humble couch."

"If this is humble, we need to re-write the dictionary."

Low-volume sounds of Beethoven's "Pathétique" seemed to be gently rising from everywhere.

The full-floor loft with its expanse of windows on the west side felt like a museum to Mitch with a long, plush white couch against the north wall, and an equally long footstool more like a short couch itself. Small marble coffee tables were built in to the couch. Sitting across from it on the south wall, the wide fireplace was more like a bonfire, but gracefully on low flame. The walls were lined with artwork, subtle ceiling light softly highlighting each one.

Mitch plopped down on the sofa.

"I need a helmet. This is like a football field."

Rebel laughed softly.

"You want a drink? A glass of wine?"

"How about an unsweetened ice tea?"

She pointed at him.

"Just like you ordered at lunch. I got it for you! With lime, right?"

"Right."

She disappeared around the corner and in less than a minute returned with his drink and a glass of white wine for herself. She slipped softly next to him at an angle so she could see him without turning her head, her legs tucked under her.

"You said your agent's giving you a week off. Then where to?"

"Canada, I think. Yeah. Somewhere still with snow so we can have lovely snow scenes, I guess. It's a winter fashion shoot for L.L. Bean. They'll want the ads and commercials all in place for Christmas."

"Skiing, do you think?"

"I don't know. That would be fun. Do you like to ski?"

"Never been. I hear folks run into trees."

"Yeah, but it's kind of like plane crashes. Not that often. You like sports though, right?"

"Yeah! I grew up in a sports-minded family. Our motto was 'If you don't shoot, you don't score.'"

They both laughed softly. Rebel studied him.

"Mitch, you look like an athlete."

"Way back. I played in high school, and small-college basketball. Did you play?"

"High school, yeah. Basketball and softball. And I grew up loving baseball, going with my dad to see the Braves."

"Oh and ugh! The Braves. The Mets' nemesis."

"You're a Mets fan?"

"Big fan. You have to be a big fan these days. Remember the great old teams while you suffer through the struggling present."

"You go to games?"

"Naw. Used to a decade ago. But work has gotten busier. And you know I have these news digests I like putting together while I watch them on TV."

"You want to go to a game? The season starts next week."

"I know. Do you go?"

"My agent's a big fan. He gives his clients season tickets."

Mitch watched her and gave a small laugh.

"What?"

"A lifelong Braves fan with Mets season tickets. What have the gods done?"

Rebel laughed out loud.

"I like the Mets!" she retorted. "But if we go see them when the Braves are in town, you won't ostracize me if I wear my Braves cap, will you?"

"Never. I'll be proud sitting next to you."

They watched each other in obvious appreciation.

"I need to check on the pasta," Rebel finally said. "You hungry?"

"I'm anxious to try your creation!"

"Come on."

They rose, and she took his hand, leading him around the corner to the dining and kitchen area. The elegant white marble dining table sat on a plush grey rug with six grey, comfortably padded dining chairs. The setting was simple white China, with two tall lighted candles centered on the table. The open kitchen with its marble tops was sparkling.

An aroma of rich garlic and basil filled the area.

"I hope you like garlic," Rebel said as she poured the pasta from its pan into a colander in the sink.

"Love it! It's gotten me through decades of pandemics!"

"Yeah, I love it, too! It's really healthy for you."

"In winter I'll eat a clove of raw garlic, usually with a sub sandwich, at lunch to keep the evil demons at bay," said Mitch.

"Really?"

"Really. A guy walked by my desk once, stopped and said, 'I smell garlic.' I said, 'That's me.' He asked. 'Lord, what do you do about dates?' I said, 'I date ladies that love garlic.' "

Rebel laughed, turned and looked at him. "Well, you picked the right lady. Bring those plates over here, will you?"

"Rebel, this smell's really delicious."

"It's my mom's recipe. Get ready for deep South."

During the meal, Rebel said she had looked at Mitch's online technology and surveillance digest.

"I don't get what's going on with Big Tech and governments," she said. "One month, some government's fining them, the next it's giving them a huge contract."

"You see exactly what's going on," Mitch responded. "It's the ultimate hate-love relationship. Or maybe hate-need relationship is more accurate. Governments are paranoid of Big Tech surveilling *them*, not so much their citizenry. But they're also paranoid the press will catch tech tapping their citizenry on behalf of business or government, so they make efforts to regulate them, then fine them from time to time for publicity sake."

"But you've got articles about governments giving them huge contracts."

"Yeah, particularly for defense, which is really a geopolitical quagmire. For example, the U.S. will almost give one major tech firm a defense cloud contract, but another big tech firm will sue. So the government will end up contracting with all five of the big tech firms. And the unfortunate reality is that our military is so huge, it needs all five.

"Other governments will try to keep up. So Big Tech ends up supplying their services to governments globally, all trying to protect themselves from each other by basically using the same tech services."

"So are they really protecting themselves?"

"That's the multi-trillion-dollar question."

Mitch began describing his limited understanding of the connections of governments, Big Tech, and weapons developers and suppliers, and how complicated it could all become due to political alliances and America's dedication to endless war. It took a while. And he suddenly became embarrassed.

"I'm sorry. I've talked too long about this."

"No, please! I want to know about this." And the almost-journalist-turned-rich-model meant it.

So Mitch kept talking. He got into the growth of surveillance in recent decades: the U.S. now with five security cameras for every American. And how the media tends to support it through crime dramas, showing how security cameras help police forces catch criminals…without ever showing how they also surveil every citizen.

Rebel said she had been reading about artificial intelligence, and experts' concerns about it taking control of every aspect of life. Mitch stressed his concerns about AI and the military and endless war, as well as its control of nuclear arsenals, with the possibility of no human being able to stop a technical glitch that could lead to nuclear war. That led them both to silent reflection.

"Technology is changing so fast," Rebel said. "There's no way government can ever keep up with regulating it. Is there?"

"That's government's history with regulating most everything," Mitch said. "Even when government really wants to."

"Tell me there's hope," Rebel said softly.

I wish I could, Mitch thought. Then he smiled at her.

"There's hope. We still have a free press." But he felt like he was lying. So he added, "Barely."

After the meal, including Rebel's homemade chocolate crème brulee, they relaxed on the couch, the classical music inviting peace. They were quiet for a while, watching the low flames in the fireplace, both with their stocking feet propped up on the long footstool. Their heads resting on the couch back, their shoulders nearly touching.

"What are you thinking?" Rebel finally asked him.

"I'm thinking how restful this place must be for you. After your long days shooting, the travel, the rush of the city itself when you're in town. Man…you can almost get lost in this couch…and the Chopin."

"So you like classical music."

"I listen to it when I curate my news digests. It's especially soothing since the news I put online…is not."

Silence.

"You're right," she said. "I'm very comfortable here. The furniture's a little fancy for me. I've a friend who was so excited to do the interior decoration, I decided to let her create. But I chose all the artwork."

Mitch gazed at the painting across from them, a brilliant yellow and gold of flames on the left side, and their reflections in water, with a stretching stone bridge on the right.

Rebel got up and walked to the end of the long couch. She reached down to its side and pressed a button. A drawer automatically opened. Mitch couldn't see what it was. The classical music stopped. Then he heard what sounded like a needle landing on a phonograph record. She has a turntable, he thought: that grand old medium folks still turn to for real music quality, and even nostalgia.

And now the soothing voice of Tony Bennett and a tinkling piano:

The way you wear your hat

The way you sip your tea

The memory of all that

No, they can't take that away from me...

Rachel was standing over him, reaching down.

"Come dance with me."

The smooth and easy trumpet sliding in.

"I'm not a very good dancer," Mitch nearly whispered.

She flexed her hand, beckoning him. He got up. They held each other, moving slowly in their stocking feet over the shiny waxed wood floor.

We may never, never meet again

On the rocky road to love

But I'll always, always keep the memory of

The way you hold your knife

The way we danced till three

The way you changed my life

No, they can't take that away from me...

When the song ended, a brief silence. Then the sound of the needle hitting the record again. And Tony's voice repeating the song.

Mitch nodded toward the painting he had been gazing at over the fireplace before Rebel turned on the music. They both spoke softly.

"That painting...isn't that Turner?"

"Yes. 'The Burning of the Houses of Lords and Commons'. From the first time I saw it, it captivated me."

"Is it an original?"

Rebel sniffed a laugh.

"I wish," she said. "The original's at the Philadelphia Museum of Art. I got an artist friend to recreate it. I think he did a great job."

"Yes, he did," Mitch said. "I like it."

Silence. Tony singing:

The way you changed my life...

"I like *you*, Mitchell," she nearly whispered.

"I like you, too, Rebel. A lot."

She looked at him. They melted into each other.

The king-sized bed seemed more like a vast cloud, and if making love is really heaven, then the night had canonized two saints.

As Mitch began to move from drowse to waking, he realized Rebel was sleeping with her head on his bare chest, his arm wrapped gently around her bare back. Her flowing hair smelled of peach shampoo seasoned slightly with garlic. He softly kissed the top of her head.

She stirred easily, then let out a soft, long breath.

"You awake?" she asked.

"I'm not sure."

They both sniffed a laugh. She looked up at him, then reached up and kissed him gently, and almost buried her head back in his chest.

They lay there in silence, both seeming to cherish the moment.

"Why would anyone ever want to leave this bed," Mitch said.

"Shall I take that as a lover's compliment...are do you want to buy the bed?"

He laughed and kissed her forehead. She looked at him. He gently put a hand to her face and slowly, softly kissed each eye. Then her waiting mouth. Then their bodies and psyches agreed again to be blessed.

The morning had seemed to quickly turn into early afternoon, the bed truly too inviting to leave.

"Your chest makes the perfect pillow," Rebel said. "Can you leave it here when you go?"

"Oh, no!" he gasped gently. "It's Hannibal Lecter's daughter!"

They both enjoyed the image. Then silence as they both gazed at the ceiling striped with shade and sunlight from the curtained window.

"Mitchell."

"Yes, m'am."

"I've a confession to make."

"You have seven husbands, one on each continent?"

She laughed softly.

"No. That's not it."

She sat up and looked at him.

"That day we met at McDonald's. I pretended I didn't know you. But I did."

Mitch watched her, wanting to hear more.

"I walked in and saw you sitting there alone, and knew immediately who you were. You look just like your picture on your column in *Center Stage*. And I got excited. I mumbled, 'Please, don't anybody sit with him.' And I hurried, got my breakfast, then tried to casually join you, and play ignorant."

"Why?"

"Well...shit...One reason is...I'm actually shy. Also, I was excited, because I really like your writing in the paper. But I was also scared.

I didn't know what you'd be like. You might have been a real asshole. Journalists can be."

"Well...I certainly can be."

"I'm sure. It goes with the territory. But when I started talking with you, you were...well...you were a strange combination...an honest journalist...and a little boy."

"Little boy!?!"

"Yes...you were. Particularly when I started to leave, and you playfully pleaded with me to call you. That tickled me. You were funny."

"Oh, it wasn't my ultra intelligence or my Brad Pitt good looks..."

Rebel didn't quite howl with laughter.

"No. It wasn't those two endearing qualities."

They laughed. She gazed at him.

"A guy's being funny...is almost salvation to a woman," she said, nearly looking through him. "And being funny AND honest...IS salvation. When you made that simple statement to me about the fashion industry being a lash on the soul. You remember that?"

Mitch watched her. Her eyes were starting to fill, and he could sense his starting too also.

"I remember saying something about the industry that moved you, but not exactly..."

"You said you knew the industry. 'I know it can be a grind,' you said. 'Even a lash on the soul...with its obsession...with physical beauty.' And I thought...god...that's exactly what it is. I want to spend time with this guy."

They watched each other like small children gazing at flames. Mitch reached up, took her in his arms. They kissed and held each other for a long time.

Eventually, Mitch whispered to her.
"Hey. You treated me to a classic meal. How about I treat you to a grubby brunch?"

"I thought you didn't want to leave this bed."

"You're right. Who delivers?"

They left the bed. Made their way to The Dutch on Sullivan Street. She had called ahead, made a reservation. They were starved, and mixed soft fits of laughter with Southern-style Eggs Benedict, country ham, and red-eye hollandaise. He thought she might have a bloody Mary. But she joined him with his iced unsweetened tea. Then he walked her back home through the radiant, breezy spring Manhattan day. They talked a while, kissed, and Mitch made his way home to work on a news digest and consider his next step with Wilmer Bracken.

A KNOCK AT THE DOOR

As he made his way up Sullivan Street, he thought about Rebel's little confession. He laughed. Then he thought about first seeing Wilmer Bracken at McDonald's. Could Bracken also have known who he was before he sat down. Could he have been setting Mitch up?

"Ohhh, Morgan," he moaned softly to himself. "Your alcoholic's ego is slipping back in. Ego-centered fear. Magnifying mind."

The reality, he thought to himself, obviously is that Wilmer Bracken is losing his memory. When Mitch first saw him, and since then, he has had problems with recognizing Mitch, and with remembering his own actions.

"You need a meeting." He had missed his regular Sunday morning gathering.

He immediately changed direction, heading to a meeting in the West Village.

At the meeting, he saw Kenneth T., who Mitch knew was a retired special forces officer. They chatted after the meeting about their sobriety. Then Mitch asked him his view of the world situation.

"We're not far from war," he said flatly. "I can feel it."

Back at his apartment, Mitch began working on his *Global Economy* digest. Sunday was usually set for nuclear arms, but he had neglected updating his economic news, so concentrated on that instead. He had 1,000 regular readers now who clicked in on Facebook alone, mostly in Asia and the Middle East, to get updated on global economics. About half that number looked at it on

LinkedIn and Univerz. At times his ego wished he had more readers. At times his sobriety was grateful for each one. This was being of service.

After placing the digest articles, he wrote his blog summarizing his view of the global economic situation. "Thick Clouds, Heavy Rain" he wrote in his blog's headline.

He went on to talk about how the world's two largest economies – the U.S. and China -- were both in trouble, and now clearly joined by a third economic force: India's concentration on tech development and trade had served it well over the last decade.

But problems persisted and seemed to be growing for all nations: climate change was abusing countries with topsy turvy weather worldwide. Storms were heavier and longer, droughts also, resulting in greater floods, wildfires, and worst of all crop failures and food shortages.

"At a time when nations should be looking to ally and coordinate efforts to help one another through this, regional military conflicts seem to sprout like fiery sores on the earth's surface," Mitch wrote. "The devastation to infrastructures leads to starvation and disease, and surely will leave civilization with a younger generation worldwide suffering from Post Traumatic Stress Disorder and brain injuries from our devastating environmental war. And crumbled economies that will affect everything from education, to jobs, to their capability to form marriages, raise families and own homes – historically the unifying fabric of a society."

Mitch paused, wondering if he was accurate or just being dramatic. Should he maybe erase that paragraph. Then he decided it felt honest. It's what his experience and research led him to believe. He left it in.

He had also asked himself, when Rebel read it, would she feel he was being honest. That surprised him. He had never considered how a lover might feel about his journalistic writing.

He breathed out heavily.

"I may be in trouble," he whispered to himself.

Then he smiled, grateful for good trouble.

He video-recorded his written blog, then put the digest on Facebook, LinkedIn, and Univerz.

Monday morning at work, Mitch received an email from Sylvia Longing, the head of WGBH-TV in Boston, Massachusetts's and one of the nation's major PBS affiliates. She advised Mitch of a private meeting at her station which would include officials of the country's major PBS stations on Wednesday morning.

"Chiefs from the biggest PBS stations in each state will meet to form a unified message to take back to their states, and to forward to Congress's conference committee currently determining the future of PBS funding," she wrote.

"Because of your consistent, concerned reporting on this issue over the years, I'm inviting you to join us."

Mitch immediately grew excited. The timing was splendid. He had already decided to go to Boston to meet in confidence with an attorney he knew about Wilmer Bracken.

He quickly responded to Longing's email, thanking her for the invitation, and that he planned to be present for the PBS meeting.

He then emailed Stan Hadley to see if Hadley could meet with him confidentially on Wednesday afternoon. Half an hour later, attorney Hadley had responded, setting a 3 pm meeting in his office.

Mitch was set, feeling grateful. He went in to his editor Abby Schulberg's office and informed her only about going to the PBS meeting. She liked the idea.

Back at his desk, Mitch was suddenly hearing again Wilmer Bracken's warning words: "We don't have much time."

Mitch grabbed his rolodex, quickly looked up Miranda McCarthy's number.

"Miranda, it's Mitchell Morgan."

"Hey, Mitch!"

"Possible I can come to your office this afternoon for a confidential meeting?"

Pause.

"Okay. 4:30?"

"See you then."

Mitch had met Miranda McCarthy some 20 years earlier in a recovery meeting. It was his first year of trying to stop drinking. She had two years sober. They learned each other were in the publishing profession – he newspaper, her books -- and immediately hit it off, becoming close friends and confidants.

She was now publisher at Heartfelt, a small romance book publisher with offices in the landmark Flatiron Building at 23rd Street. Her publishing background was with mystery novels. But when another global health pandemic a few years earlier sent the economy, and the publishing industry, into another tailspin, she decided she wanted to eat, and took the top spot at Heartfelt.

She stared with both amazement and some obvious fear at Mitch. He had just summarized his relationship with Wilmer Bracken, including pitching her the memoir and the top-secret nuclear report.

"We publish romances for a mushy female audience," Miranda moaned, unconsciously pulling on a strand of her shoulder-length sandy-colored hair. "This is intrigue and assassinations, Mitch."

"Yeah, and I write about the entertainment business. But, Miranda, this is history, of international concern, and a blockbuster. Spread your wings and help educate the world while you make a lot of money!"

Miranda's clear blue eyes studied him.

"It *will* make a lot of money, won't it."
"Including film rights."

She picked up the memoir manuscript and re-read the first few pages. She set it down and looked at Mitch. Then she picked up the phone.

"Who're you calling?" he asked.

"Our lawyer."

"Oh, fuck, Miranda! He'll say no!"

"SHE…will give me her honest opinion."

The attorney agreed to meet with them in Miranda's office the next day.

These "extracurricular" activities meant Mitch now would actually have two deadline nights. Not only the regular Tuesday night, but now tonight, when he would have to work late editing other editors' columns and setting the news layout. But before he even did that, he sat and wrote his column updating the Congressional arts funding issue…but not mentioning the private PBS meeting Wednesday. He would only say that arts organizations nationwide were communicating with Congress in an effort for a positive outcome to the funding question.

His phone rang.

"Mitch, this is Sidney Golden. You're working late."

"You know us journalists, Sid. Ever serving the public."

Golden laughed gratuitously then made his point: "We've reached a stalemate in our negotiations with the Philharmonic."

Golden was the attorney for Local 802 of the American Federation of Musicians, the union representing instrumentalists throughout New York City, including the major classical music venues. He was referring to the venerated New York Philharmonic Symphony Orchestra, now 200 years old, which performed at the globally famous Lincoln Center for the Performing Arts in Manhattan.

"Sidney…are you saying 'strike'?"

"Not yet," said the hoarse-voiced Golden. "The orchestra members will have to vote, and will tomorrow. But I wanted to give you a heads-up."

"I really appreciate it. Are you issuing a statement to that effect?"

"I just emailed you our press release. Call me if you need more."

Mitch checked his email. Local 802's release was there. From its opening statement, it wanted to punch with power:

AFM Local 802 represents thousands of highly skilled musicians who drive New York City's thriving cultural and tourism economy. Its members — who perform on Broadway, at Lincoln Center, Carnegie Hall and Radio City, in recording studios, as teaching artists, on late-night TV shows and in other televised bands, in hotels, clubs, festivals and venues across NYC — are protected by collective bargaining agreements ensuring proper classification, fair treatment and a living wage.

The release then went into what management at the Philharmonic allegedly wasn't willing to provide its musicians: "a reasonable wage increase to fight inflation, and humane health insurance. This shows not only a lack of respect for these professional artists, but also for the faithful audiences that attend to hear their dynamic performances."

Now Mitch, who for years had covered the contract scene, would have to call Teresa Flanagan, communications director at the Philharmonic, to get their side of the story.

"Here we go," thought Mitch. "Always on deadline."

He decided he wanted to call Rebel. He got her voicemail, her soft voice sounding like a sensual yogi leading a meditation.

"Hey, Rebel. It's Mitch. I've suddenly gotten avalanched with busy. I'm gonna have a late deadline both tonight and Tuesday night. Then I fly out early Wednesday. Can maybe we have dinner together Thursday night? Let me know. I'll make a reservation. Wish I could think of something funny to say…anyway. I think I'm seeing you everywhere. And that's not funny. That's delightful. Bye."

Mitch finally stepped into his dark studio just after 10 pm, flipping the light, locking the door, and flopping down on the living room couch, sipping on a hot herbal tea.

A knock at the door. What the hell?

"Who is it?"

"Mister Morgan, we're with the federal government. We'd like to speak to you."

A cold fear swept through Mitch. A quick prayer. To open the door or not? He cracked it open.

Two men dressed in dark suits stood there, serious faces, each holding out an identification card toward Mitch.

"We're with the Central Intelligence Agency."

Mitch watched them. Faith and sober action, he told himself.

"You know my name," Mitch said. "I don't know yours. Could you hold those IDs a little closer."

They were officers Madison and Gonzalez within the CIA's Directorate of Operations.

"Okay," Mitch said. "What's up?"

"Do you know this man?"

Officer Madison held up his smartphone with a CIA photo of Wilmer Bracken.

"Why?" asked Mitch.

"We have reason to believe you are communicating with him about classified CIA information," Gonzalez said gruffly.

Mitch watched them.

"That looks like a CIA photo you're showing me. Is it?"

"Yes," said Madison.

"So...is this guy a CIA agent?"

"We believe you know he is a CIA officer."

"Well...if he is...why don't you ask him what he's doing with any classified CIA information?"

"We're concerned you might reveal such information to the public. It's classified. And you're a journalist. It would be illegal for you to do so."

Mitch was feeling that ego-centered fear combined with that old competitive athleticism fire up.

"You're right. I *am* a journalist. And I believe that, according to my Constitutional right to freedom of the press, I have the freedom to interview employees of the United States Government…like you… about their activities. So the public will know. Hold on."

Mitch stepped quickly to his close-by writing desk, picked up one of his press notebooks and a pen, and moved back to the cracked door. He opened the door a little farther so the agents could see him begin to write in the notebook.

"So…officers Madison and Gonzalez…let's go on the record, and you tell me and the American public what you're actually involved in here?"

He looked up. To his surprise, the two agents looked at each other, and began walking toward the elevator.

"We'll be back in touch," Madison said.

"You do that!" Mitch called out, slamming the door.

He stumbled to the couch, dropping on to it, breathing heavily, sweating.

Had he actually just challenged two CIA agents? And had they actually walked away? He breathed in deeply, and breathed out a whispering prayer.

He lay back his head against the couch top. Exhausted, he began to steadily deep-breathe, silently reviewing the Twelve Steps to help him remember there's a greater power than himself, than even the CIA.

Should he call or text Wilmer to warn him? No. Wilmer would be the first to know how the CIA works…if he could remember. Then he decided to text Bracken.

Just was visited by two of your former workers. They left abruptly when I told them I wanted to interview them for a story.

A few minutes later, a brief understated response:

You must be careful.

No shit, thought Mitch. But now Bracken is aware the Agency was getting more active. And his older warning repeated its flashing through Mitch's mind:

"We don't have much time."

Mitch thought about texting Bracken that he had found a publisher to pitch his story, but then decided against it. He'd tell him when he saw him face to face, hopefully Thursday.

His smartphone chimed. It was Rebel.

"I tried to call earlier," she said softly.

"Boy, am I glad to hear your soothing voice," Mitch said.

"You all right?" she asked.

"Just a blistering day and night, trying to keep up with the world," he said, and found himself laughing in nervous release.

"You said you're flying out Wednesday?"

"Yeah. The major PBS stations are meeting privately in Boston, wanting to organize an approach to Congress to save their funding. I've been invited to attend."

"Mitch, that sounds like a great compliment."

"Yeah, it is, isn't it. I guess I'm the Clark Kent of the cultural world. Fighting for truth, justice, and the American way."

Silence.

"Oh," Mitch said. "A little much, eh?"

Rebel started laughing.

Silence.

"So you want to have dinner Thursday?" she asked.

"That would make my week," Mitch replied.

"Mine, too." she said.

THE LAWYERS

As Mitch opened his door to leave Tuesday morning, a card fell from the door's crack. Officer Madison had come back and left a business card. So, intelligence and surveillance had become so widespread and accepted in America that now the government's clandestine agency left business cards. But the card didn't hint of clandestine. It displayed the agency's crest with text:

CIA Directorate of Operations

Edward Madison, Officer

New York Office: 111 Eighth Avenue

New York, NY 10011

212-385-0118

Mitch stepped to his desk and put the card in the top drawer.

The early-morning meeting with Miranda and her attorney was logically intense. Bina Saphire was short and stocky, with calculating brown eyes and an alto voice that could host a radio talk show. She had three decades of legal experience in publishing, could recite law like a rabbi could quote the Torah, with interpretation.

"The federal government will come after the company and you, Miranda, if you publish just one of these documents," Saphire said. "They'll argue that your actions are criminal, will fight to ban either or both books, and try to put you in prison."

"What about Mitch?" Miranda asked solemnly.

Saphire responded to Miranda, but she was looking at Mitch as she spoke.

"If they find out you provided the manuscripts to the publisher, they'll come after you. But, honestly, that's not my concern. You're not my client."

"The CIA officers knocked on my door last night," Mitch said.

The room swelled with silence. Then Saphire:

"So what happened?"

"They started to ask me about Bracken, and I pulled the journalist on them. I took out a notebook and pen and said I wanted to interview them. To my surprise, they left. But one came back and left his business card in my door. I guess my invitation to call him and tell all. Which journalists don't do, except in their news stories."

Silence. Then Miranda:

"Bina, I took both manuscripts home last night and read them through. I understand what you're saying. But I believe this is a rare chance for me, and for this publishing company, to print something the public deserves to know about. And I think it will help us finally make a big profit for the first time."

"That profit may get eaten up with legal expenses," said Saphire.

Miranda stared at her. Then she started to smile. And Saphire began to smile.

"Okay," the attorney said. "Looks like I'm going to have to research past cases the feds have brought on behalf of the CIA."

She looked at both of them.

"I'll say one thing. You're lucky we're not in Great Britain. There you would have to prove you're innocent. Here, at least, they'll have to prove you're guilty."

"Guilty we've informed taxpayers what the government's been doing with their taxes? And that their actions have been illegal," said Mitch.

"Let me take a look at the manuscripts. Then I can better determine that."

"Look at them here, please, Bina," Miranda said. "We can't afford any other eyes anywhere seeing these."

"I'll be back in the morning," Saphire said.

Mitch felt grateful. He had gotten through Tuesday deadline night without any glitches and was home by 11 pm. He had an hour-long Wednesday 7:59 am flight to Boston, and should be able to make the PBS meeting, scheduled to start at 10.

Lying in bed, his head swam with faces he needed to pray for. The process began to relax him, and he ever so slowly drifted into sleep.

He hated to fly, so rarely did. The hassle with TSA ever since 9/11 had always stressed him. And it did again on what was actually a lovely sunny Wednesday morning. But once past the security check, he was able to settle into the morning papers, including his own, reviewing the articles and his column with fresh eyes.

He wasn't able to walk into WGBH-TV's PBS meeting until 10:30. An attendant led him through the impressive GBH (the TV station's on-air brand name) headquarters to the auditorium and its two tiers of seating. Most of the cream-back seats with comfy blue cushions were filled in the first tier, some 50 people representing a PBS major station in each state.

On the grey-floored stage, looking down at them from the dais, was GBH's Sylvia Longing. A large screen behind her highlighted a graphic of proposed PBS funding which was before the Congressional conference committee currently determining the PBS stations' future.

She saw Mitch walking in, looking to take a seat just behind the others. She paused in her talk, then said, "Folks, joining us right now is Mitchell Morgan from *Center Stage* in New York. I invited him to this private meeting because he's been a mainstay of reporting on PBS activities, particularly Congressional funding. His reports have always been fair and accurate. And I think what he writes about us here today will be vital on getting the word out on what we'll be communicating to Congress."

Heads turned, smiles, and some light applause.

"So, if you will," continued Longing, "when you speak, could you say your name and which state and station you represent. It will help him in his reporting, and also help readers to see how we're representing the entire country."

The meeting went straight through until 1:30, when they broke for lunch. Mitch went up to talk to Longing.

"Sylvia, I want to thank you for inviting me," Mitch said. "I've a lot of meat here for a good article, and probably a column as well. I've got to go. Will you email me your final statement and any other material you all decide to send the conference committee in Washington."

She said she would.

Stan Hadley grew up a Massachusetts farm boy, family raising hay in Middlesex County in the state's northwest. But he outgrew farming, almost outgrowing the horses the hay fed. Before he left high school he measured in at six feet six inches and 265 pounds of muscle from tossing hay bales. And in high school, the football coaches learned he was also fast, quick, smart, and was a linebacker that could crush a running back with brutal candor.

Catholic boy, he went on to star at Boston College, was drafted by the New York Jets, where he started as a rookie. But gradually booze, and then cocaine, tackled *him* with brutal candor. He found himself in recovery, and one night sitting next to Mitchell Morgan in Mitch's Greenwich Village home group. He eventually asked Mitch to sponsor him, and together they walked through the Twelve Steps.

Stan got sober, learned how to live sober, and life began to change. He applied for law school at his alma mater, was accepted, and returned to Boston. For a number of years now, his practice had concentrated on recovered felons, helping them get paroled, working, and renewing their right to vote.

Mitch couldn't help himself. When first sitting down in Stan's paper-stacked office, he automatically returned to his old sponsor role.

"You still going to meetings?"

"At least five a week," Stan said, smiling. "Got two sponsees. And here I guess you could say I'm involved in love and service, although I get paid for it."

"Worthy faith and action," Mitch responded, and they both grinned.

"What brings you from the city of a million attorneys to me?"

Mitch began filling Stan in on his meeting and beginning to work with Wilmer Bracken. He pulled out copies of Bracken's memoir and the confidential nuclear weapons report. He added that he had a book publisher in New York willing to publish both documents.

Stan read the first few pages of each one, then looked up at Mitch.

"You're driving a truckload of danger here, buddy."

"Don't I know it," Mitch responded. "What I don't know are the legal specifics. The attorney for the publisher said she and her company would be charged by the government; and the publisher, if convicted would go to jail. But I'm not with that company, and not represented by that attorney, or any attorney. And journalists don't assume. What can the government do to me?"

"You picked a bad time to challenge Washington," Stan said. "Congress has been moving more and more toward fascism ever since Trump."

"Yeah, he wanted to be a dictator. Biden just wanted to stay an oligarch. And Obama before them wanted to put a Pulitzer Prize-winning reporter in prison for protecting a source. That was an effort to put fear in all journalists."

"Well, Trump and Biden are dust now, and Obama's a distant memory," Stan said. "But it's gotten worse. The current president…"

"…who's another oligarch moving toward fascist," Mitch interrupted.

"…who's an oligarch moving toward fascist," Stan repeated. "But, as you probably know, Congress last session passed legislation, and the oligarch-fascist signed it, that makes the Espionage Act look like a misdemeanor.

"Now almost anything with a government seal on it is classified with criminal punishments for revealing it. And what's in these two documents ranges from highly classified to top secret. If a jury finds you guilty of breaking a law by releasing these to the public, you can kiss your freedom goodbye, probably for decades."

"What about the Constitutional rights to freedom of the press and freedom of expression?"

"What about them? The government's trying to abolish them."

"But will a judge, and more so a jury, abolish them?"

"That's an argument we'll have to make and see how they respond."

"We?" Mitch smiled at Stan.

The former pro linebacker took a deep breath, looked at his former sponsor, and tried not to smile. But he did, barely.

"Yeah…we. The good news is, if you get convicted, I'm great at getting felons paroled, and getting back their right to vote."

"I'll option for not getting convicted."

Stan watched him.

"Who's the publisher and attorney?"

Mitch told him.

"Ol' Miranda," said Stan, smiling. "What a sweetheart. I still remember in one of my real early days getting sober, sitting alone before a meeting, looking down depressed. She walked by, stopped, looked at me and said, 'If nobody's told you they love you today, well the higher power and I do."

"Place for her in heaven," Mitch said.

"I don't know Bina Saphire, but I sure know of her. She's in every law school's textbook on contracts."

"She said she's going to research the Justice Department's past cases involving the CIA."

"That's a good start," Stan said. "I'll give her a call. I can hold on to these two documents?"

"Like they're your passport to salvation. Please keep 'em close."

Stan nodded. They watched each other.

"One other thing you need to know," Mitch said. "Two CIA agents came to see me at home late Monday night."

Stan's eyes grew more focused. Mitch explained how they asked about Bracken, but Mitch had deflected that with saying he had the press freedom to interview them, started to try, and they left.

"They said they'd be back," Mitch said.

"I'll bet they did," Stan said flatly. He looked up, thinking, maybe even praying. Then: "You need to be careful. You have a weapon?"

"Just the Constitution."

"That may not be enough."

"It'll have to be. I'm a writer, not a fighter."

"Did you inform Bracken about them."

"I texted him. He texted back. He agrees with you. He told me I needed to be careful. Which I already figured out."

"They'll go after him."

"He knows that…if he can remember. But he seems to have taken care of himself so far. Stan, I realized a few days ago a guy was following me. I surprised him by taking his photo on my smartphone, and he took off. I showed the photo to Bracken. A couple of days later I noticed the guy wasn't following me anymore. I told Bracken. He said I wouldn't have to worry about him anymore. 'I've taken care of it,' he said. That's all he'd tell me."

Stan studied him.

"So…Bracken either complained to the CIA…not likely, I think. Or he found and complained to the guy following you."

"You think he may have killed him? Disposed of the body somewhere?"

"Maybe."

"Well…Agents Madison and Gonzalez didn't ask about him."

"Maybe you didn't give them time to. Or maybe they were going to visit Bracken and ask him."

"I plan on seeing him Thursday."

"Let me know how that goes."

"Okay."

They studied each other.

"How long you in town?" Stan asked. "Can you have dinner with us tonight? Meet my wife and kids?"

"Thanks, Stan, but next visit I guess. I've got a plane out tonight."

"Maybe you can make it up for a weekend soon. Stay with us."

"You think maybe I'll have to?"

"Maybe."

Stan didn't quite crush Mitch's back as they hugged goodbye.

MEMORY

Thursday morning at work, Mitch's email check showed a long missive from Sylvia Longing detailing the PBS stations' statement to Congress's conference committee and each station's Congressional delegation. That with Mitch's notes would make for both a good front page story and also his weekly column next week.

And he also clicked on an email from Sidney Golden, who said Local 802 had delayed a strike vote, deciding to try one more negotiation session with the Philharmonic management. That would be Friday. Golden promised to let Mitch know the result.

His smartphone binged with a text from Rebel.

"You've got to be exhausted after deadline and the Boston trip. So let's not go out to eat. Why don't you come by tonight at 6 and I'll have dinner waiting, and we both can relax."

"Smooth talker!" he texted back. "See thee at 6. And thank you."

She binged back a heart icon.

Mitch wrote and filed his story on the PBS stations' meeting, and their communication to Congress. Then he decided to take the afternoon off, save his column for Friday. He grabbed a tuna sub and soda, and after devouring them, headed to see Wilmer Bracken.

"I have a publisher who has agreed to publish both of your manuscripts," Mitch told him.

Wilmer sat without speaking, letting that thought settle in. He looked at Mitch and nodded.

"Is it better if I don't tell you who that is yet?"

Bracken nodded.

"When the publisher is ready, I'll have you meet, and with their attorney too. They're taking a big risk. You know that."

119

Bracken nodded.

"Okay," Mitch said. "I'll let you know when. And they know what we know: we don't have much time."

"I'm starting to remember a little," Bracken said.

Mitch watched him, surprised.

"Well," said Mitch, "that's good. You had written that the doctors and the medications hadn't worked."

"They hadn't. Then last week, I saw a new doctor."

He got up, went into his bathroom, and returned holding a prescription bottle. He showed it to Mitch. The medical name meant nothing to the journalist. It was long, and Mitch thought it might be a combination of drugs.

"The doctor said it's a new drug they're still testing. I've been taking it for a week. I've been reading my memoir. And I'm starting to remember what I'm reading. Not a lot, but some. And I remembered you when I opened the door."

"Wilmer…that sounds like a helluva good start."

"We'll see."

"Yes. We will," smiled Mitch.

They were sitting on the couch, watching each other.

"Wilmer, do you remember me texting you earlier this week? About the two CIA agents who came to see me?"

"Do you remember their names?" Bracken asked.

Mitch smiled at the irony of Bracken asking Mitch about his own memory.

"Yes. I do. Agents Madison and Gonzalez."

Bracken thought. It didn't seem to register. He took his notebook and wrote the names down.

"Anyway," said Mitch, "I seemed to have actually startled them when I said I wanted to interview them. They looked at each other, then quickly turned and began leaving. And Madison said they'd be back. After I slammed the door on them, he left a business card in my door."

"Yes. They'll be back. You must be careful."

"I understand."

They watched each other.

"Wilmer, do you remember our talking about the guy that was following me?"

Wilmer thought. Then nodded yes. Mitch was surprised he didn't have to refer to his notebook.

"I remember," Bracken said. "You don't have to worry about him anymore."

Mitch rustled in his seat, getting perturbed.

"Yeah, you told me that. You said you had taken care of it. What does that mean, you took care of it?"

"I took care of it," Bracken said flatly, as if it was the end of the conversation.

"No, Wilmer, that's not enough. I need to know more."

"No. You don't."

Mitch studied him. Bracken's expression was calm but determined. It was clear he wasn't going to say more.

"So what do I do if Agents Madison and Gonzalez come back and ask me about this guy?"

"Did they ask you about me?"

"Yes. They showed me a CIA photo of you, said they believed I was communicating with you about classified material."

"What did you say?"

"That's when I turned the tables and said I was going to interview them."

"So you didn't talk about me?"

"No."

"Good."

Bracken looked away, thinking.

"If they ask you again about me or this guy, tell them they have to talk to me."

Mitch watched him.

"Have they talked with you?"

"I don't remember if they have. I'll have to look in my notes."

Mitch nodded.

"But," Bracken added, "if they come back, you don't have to say anything to them. Tell them to come talk to me."

"You figure they've been following you, yes?"

"Probably. I'm sure someone has been…I'll need to check my notes."

Bracken let out a deep breath.

"You seem tired," Mitch said.

"Yes."

"And I'm tired. I've got more questions I'd like to ask. More things I'd like to know. But later, I guess."

"All you need to know is in the memoir."

They watched each other.

"I'm gonna go," Mitch said. "Text me if you need me."

Bracken nodded. Wrote in his notebook.

Mitch found himself reaching out again to shake Bracken's hand. Wilmer took it. Then Mitch rose and left.

Mitch couldn't help himself. He was starting more and more to pause and look around as he walked, checking to see if someone was following him. But as he made his way to Rebel's, he couldn't tell.

She was shining.

"Aw, you. You look exhausted."

He was. Standing at the open door, she reached up, embracing him, just holding him, as if her electric energy would heal him. And maybe it was. Mitch thought how he had never felt so loved so quickly and deeply by anyone.

Mitch was in some strange vast room filled with documents. Suddenly he saw Bracken moving slowly, sneaking to a desk. A woman was sitting, typing on her laptop. Bracken was grabbing her now from behind, his arms around her head. It was clear he was about to snap her head, breaking her neck.

"Wilmer! No!" Mitch shouted.

Then he woke up. He was on Rebel's long couch, his head resting on its back. Rebel was seated next to him and facing him, her legs folded under her. She was staring at him sensitively.

"I…must have…fallen asleep," Mitch mumbled.

"You dropped almost right off. I went in to get you a tea, and when I came back, you had ascended." She was smiling.

"I'm sorry."

"Don't be. Who's Wilmer?"

"Who?"

"Wilmer. In your dream you shouted, 'Wilmer! No!' "

"I did?"

She nodded.

"Wilmer? You got me. Must be my imaginary friend from when I was a kid."

"Oh, wow! Let me analyze you! What was he doing in your dream?"

Mitch studied her. Then he smiled.

"What are you, with the Gestapo? No brainwashing here!"

"Aw, Mitchell. Let me have a little fun!"

"Okay. Come here and let me hold you."

She moved close to him and he embraced her.

"Man, that was kind of you to let me rest my eyes for a little while."

"That's me. Little Miss Wonderful. Actually, you can sleep here all you want."

They watched each other with delight. Kissed. He held her.

Nearby he saw a geopolitics magazine, and next to that a book on yoga and another, David McCullough's bio of Harry Truman.

"You amaze me," Mitch said.

"Why?"

"I remember you had a magazine on geopolitics when we met. But you also had a copy of *Vogue* with you on the cover. I look around here, and I don't see one fashion magazine."

She let out a near frustrated sigh.

"Oh, Mitchell. That's work. I don't want to even think about that when I'm home."

"No need to feed the old ego that you're an amazing success?"

"The first couple of years I needed that. Not now. Now I seem to be getting hungrier and hungrier with journalistic interests. Like geopolitics. In fact, I think the world's gotten to such a frightening state, everybody better get focused on the world before their leaders destroy it."

He studied her. She turned and looked at him.

"You ever wish you'd become a journalist?" he asked.

"Sometimes."

"I bet you'd be a dandy."

"Hey. You're a news editor. You're not supposed to be biased."

They both laughed lightly, then sat, adoring each other.

She gave him a quick kiss and scooted to her feet, reaching out her hand.

"C'mon. You'd better like pizza."

He managed a bad Marlon Brando imitation.

"That sounds like an offer I can't refuse."

After the meal and being close to Rebel, Mitch was re-energized. They made love with intense care, seeming to savor every breath, every touch.

As Rebel slept, Mitch lay awake. How the wicked night seems to wait patiently for you, he thought. Then, just when you need to rest, it flashes on the blinding lights of responsibility, of fearful possibilities. What choice but to pray.

After some moments of honest prayer, he drifted off, feeling blessed in holding the soft, sensitive sleeping woman next to him.

Friday work began with the usual checking for news stories to "fill the buckets". Then Mitch began his column. He opened with a brief history of the Public Broadcasting Service, emphasizing its educational importance to the nation. Then he moved into an overview of the need for PBS today when solid teaching and news reporting were so vital for their nation that seemed to be growing more and more authoritarian. Next, he summarized this week's PBS stations' meeting in Boston, analyzing its importance in uniting the stations nationwide to speak as one voice. He linked the column to his news story on that Boston meeting.

After he went through it again, editing, and finishing, he gave a brief nod.

"Good job, Great Spirit," he whispered. He filed the column and forwarded it to Connie Van Meador for layout.

As his computer clock clicked on 4:25, he was thinking about Rebel. They had agreed to meet for dinner at Pappa's Taverna on MacDougal at 7 pm. That would allow Mitch to hit his regular 6 pm Friday meeting on Sullivan Street, leave a little early, and make the easy walk to the restaurant.

His phone rang.

"Mitch, this is Sid Golden."

Oh…shit! In his end-of-week weariness, he had completely blanked out the Friday Philharmonic negotiations.

"Sid, please don't tell me I'm gonna have to announce bad news to the world."

"I call in good cheer," the hoarse voice countered. "Local 802 has reached a tentative contract agreement with the Philharmonic."

"Oh, thank you, you saintly musicians! I was afraid…"

"Nothing to fear. I think our members will be happy with the contract's specifics. We'll mail them out over the weekend, and hopefully they'll approve it next week."

"What delightful items can you provide that I can share with our readers?"

"I'm emailing you the goodies. Then I'll report back when we get results on the vote."

"Bless you, Sid."

"I can use it. Talk soon."

Mitch got the email. His article included the major points of the contract, then he analyzed what the pact's approval would mean to a positive cultural economy in New York City. The musicians at the Philharmonic not striking meant that the musicians at the city's other major cultural venues – from The New York City Ballet to Broadway – would not have to honor the strike. It also meant that the other unions like Actors Equity Association, i.e., Broadway and Off-Broadway and Off-Off-Broadway actors, would not have to honor the strike, walk away from work and begin picketing.

"Consider the lights being dimmed from Lincoln Center to the Great White Way. For months," Mitch wrote. "That alone should tell you that millions of dollars will keep flowing into the city that otherwise could cost not only producers and artists, but the businesses that profit from tourism and the continual flow of audiences. That means everything from hotels to restaurants, to stores where those folks shop. And the city's receiving sales taxes from all that.

"But the musicians still need to vote on the new pact. The results should be in by next week."

He was through with his article by 5:30. Then he left for his meeting.

At Pappa's, Mitch savored his Faroe Islands wild salmon while Rebel complimented her brined half-roasted chicken in between sharing scenes from the Truman bio.

As she'd lean over in her bright white chair with slender mahogany arms, Mitch would lean back against the blue high-back booth seat, simply admiring her beauty and intelligence.

Finally Rebel stopped and gazed at Mitch with a quizzical expression.

"Mitchell, are you even listening to me?"

"Every word, my dear. I'm entranced by your magic. And I'm grateful to be recalling Truman's wonderful story."

"Am I hearing that you already read the book?"

"Yes and no. I listened to McCullough read the book on my old Sony Walkman back when. I'd lie in bed at night and go to sleep listening. Then the next night I'd run it back to the last thing I remembered hearing, and keep moving forward."

"So I'm not boring you?"

"Rebel, I admire Truman. I think he was an exceptional president. And McCullough won the Pulitzer for his bio, and I loved the writing, and his reading it. But hearing you helped me recall those stories I had heard McCullough read years back."

"Okay. That's good. I tell you, when I was at Mizzou, I went to Independence to see Truman's presidential library and museum. I fell in love with him and…"

"…and I'm falling in love with you."

Silence. Rebel blinked at him, her cheeks starting to turn pink. Then her eyes began to fill.

"Rebel, I didn't mean to upset you."

"I'm not upset…I'm feeling really loved."

She reached over, and he took her hand. They gazed at each other. Then she smiled impishly.

"It's my cooking, isn't it?"

"Well…I really like your cooking…"

"It's my brilliant understanding of geopolitics?"

"Well, you do have a brill…"

"It's my flashy apartment."

"Well…I like your apartment, but…"

She leaned close and whispered:

"It's my body and my wild, passionate lovemaking."

Mitch started laughing, then she started laughing. Then they both just smiled and gazed at each other.

"What about *my* wild, passionate lovemaking?" Mitch whispered back.

Rebel slumped and stared at him, trying not to smile.

"Meh."

Mitch stuck his thumb and forefinger in his water glass and flicked a stream of droplets at her.

The weekend was simply splendid. On Saturday they journeyed uptown to the Museum of Modern Art which featured a new exhibition of Cezanne's works. Then they toured the permanent Impressionist rooms. They leaned against each other, admiring Van Gogh's "The Starry Night".

"That really belongs in my living room," she whispered in Mitch's ear.

"Damn! I should have brought my overcoat."

She laughed and hugged him.

They looked through the bookshop before leaving and Mitch bought a book of Van Gogh for her.

As they made their way out of the museum, she began softly singing Don McLean's "Starry, Starry Night". Mitch joined her. He was a bit flat, but as lovers do, she ignored it.

They went to bed early, laughing and loving and finally sleeping. Then the same on Sunday morning, and surprised themselves to learn it was suddenly 4 in the afternoon.

"You hungry?" Mitch asked her.

"I'm starvin', Marvin'!"

They went back to The Dutch for the Eggs Benedict. She sipped a white wine and he had iced tea.

"Mitchell, do you never drink wine?"

"No. I don't drink any alcohol. I'm allergic. It makes me break out in handcuffs."

She laughed.

"Well, that's cool that you take care of yourself. Most of the folks I deal with in the fashion business AT LEAST drink. And engage in the recreational drugs that seem to eventually turn un-recreational. I've got two old friends who don't drink, but they're both in AA."

"Well, I've good news for you, Rebel. You now have a lover who's in AA."

"Really?"

"Really."

"How long?"

"Twenty years."

"Really!?! Well, congratulations. You must be proud."

"I'm grateful."

"Grateful…okay. That makes sense."

She looked out past Mitch, now with a bit of sadness.

"What is it, Rebel?"

"I wish…I wish my dad could get sober."

"Oh…Is it bad?"

"Well…it's not bad. It's sad. He hasn't been happy for a long time. He's been successful somehow at his business…but not at home."

"Hmm. A 'functional alcoholic'?"

"What is that?"

"Well, I'm not sure what it is exactly to others. I know what it means to me: It's someone who can function at his job. But when he gets home, he disappears into the bottle."

She gazed at him, tears forming in her eyes.

"That's him," she said. "I don't know how to help him."

"We have to want help, it seems. Otherwise, we tend to run from it. When you're with him, all you can really do is be honest with him. Look, I'll get you some literature to read. Maybe that will help you."

"Thank you, Mitchell." She reached over, took his hand, kissed it softly, holding it to her cheek.

He smiled.

"Want to go back to my place?" she asked softly.

"I feel like I need to get caught up on one of my news digests."

"You can get on my computer and do that, can't you?"

"Well, yes. I can. It usually takes a couple of hours."

"Good! I can do yoga and read. Then maybe we can…mess around."

"You're an evil woman, Rebel Daley."

She playfully acted hurt.

"But you're *my* evil woman!"

Lovers can laugh at the silliest thing as if it's the funniest joke in history. And they laughed.

Back at Rebel's, while she practiced yoga in the bedroom, Mitch sat at the dining table on her laptop, working on his *Global Law* digest.

It had become clearer and clearer as he had curated stories over the last couple of years that authoritarian governments were spreading: Asia, the Middle East, Africa, South and Central America had a history of them, but now dictators were becoming more established in what Mitch called the world's "alleged democracies". That included the European Union and America. And that was the crux of

130

stories he placed tonight, showing how dictators solidified power through the laws they passed.

He did his best to summarize this in his blog, and connect the dots:

In Asia, the coronavirus pandemic a decade ago basically destroyed China's thriving economy, led to great youth unemployment, then in mid-decade the Belt and Road Initiative fizzled, leading to President Xi's downfall. That, along with Putin's assassination in Russia, evolved to that region's falling into even more dictatorial hands, even greater citizen repression, and a division in what had been a growing China-Russia cooperation.

A greater danger appears, however, to be in Europe, where the growth of authoritarian regimes has led to spreading emphasis on isolation, threatening the stability of the European Union. It's difficult to say the union will be able to hold together through another global economic meltdown.

The greatest danger, of course, is in North America. Canada has devolved from a liberal government with broad global cooperation to a more conservative, if not right-wing, controlled state. And the United States, which has touted itself as a democracy while for decades being an oligarchy, is suffering its continued devolution. It had survived Trump's effort at a dictatorship, and since has slowly turned more authoritarian. Now we've seen a breakup within both the belligerent right and the oligarchic centrists. The two major parties have been in chaos, leading to a small revival of third parties.

Meanwhile a mainly uneducated and fearful public has resulted in barely half of eligible voters actually casting votes. States have sent more and more fascist faces to Congress. And the once-oligarchic president has been taking actions and also signing laws to increase surveillance and slowly dissolve individual rights. She has continued the increase of weapons production – including nuclear weapons – and their sale to foreign countries. Meanwhile she tries to faintly cover her tracks by supporting meager funding of cultural institutions.

Mitch thought of his earlier conversation with Rebel, and closed the blog saying, "Is there hope? Yes. As long as there is a free press. And there is one. Barely."

He was going to file the digest on Facebook, LinkedIn, and Univerz. But he stopped, looking out and thinking. He got up, grabbed the laptop and walked to the bedroom.

Rebel was sitting up on the bed, her back resting against the padded white headboard. She was over halfway through the Truman bio.

She looked up at Mitch who was standing in the doorway. She smiled.

"You done?"

He watched her, then smiled.

"Do you want to read my blog?

"Did you put it online?"

"Not yet. I want you to read it. Everybody needs an editor. Put an editing touch to it."

She grimaced.

"Mitchell...I haven't even written an article or column since college. And that was college. You're New York, and writing to a global audience."

"At least look at it. Give me your honest view."

She beamed. Held out her arms to receive the laptop. He handed it to her and stretched out next to her on the bed.

"Tell me if you think there's something I should change. Or add."

She began reading. Her green eyes glowed with more than excitement, Mitch thought. They gazed with a grateful feeling of her being trusted.

She finished.

"Wow," she almost whispered. "I call that a real overview."

Then she looked at him with a small wince.

"Promise you won't be mad if I suggest something?"

"I got sober through a program of suggestions. Please do."

He could see she wasn't sure what he meant, but she moved ahead.

"Where you write about the state of the U.S...."

"Yeah."

"I think you should say something about the engrained military-industrial complex. Just to let the reader know it has a serious effect on government policy, and their lives."

"Okay. Write it."

"Mitchell…"

"Write what you just said. Let the reader know."

She gazed at him as if he had just said, "Arise and walk."

"Okay, buster. But I'm glad you're an editor."

"Shut up and educate the reader, lady."

She turned, seemed to re-read his paragraph on Canada and America. Then she slowly began typing. She stopped, re-read what she wrote. Made a couple of changes. Then quickly, as if wanting to get rid of it, turned the laptop toward him.

He read what she wrote. He smiled.

"Okay. Good. It's accurate, it's tight, and fits in the flow of the column…but Eisenhower has only one 's'."

"Ohh…shit!"

He clicked the laptop, making the small change.

"There. Well done. It makes the blog better."

She frowned at him.

"You're just trying to make me feel good."

"My dear, my just being here makes you feel good."

She laughed and hit his arm.

"But this is journalism we're talking about. And it's MY blog. It had better be accurate, tight, and flow."

She gave him a hug and watched with delight as he placed the digest on the three online sites. He decided he'd wait until tomorrow night to add his blog video.

SETTING THE MEETING

Mitch rose early Monday while Rebel still slept. He left, made his way to his apartment to clean up and put on fresh clothes. Then he sauntered through Washington Square Park, on his way to work. He stopped briefly, sitting on a park bench, studied a group of some ten people maneuvering through Tai Chi on the park grass.

As he watched, he thought of Rebel meditating, then of her magic eyes as she wrote on her laptop. He gave a small prayer of gratitude for her. He silently asked for guidance in living sober "through Your Monday, to do Your will, and connect the dots in being of love and service to all."

He briefly thought that "to all" may sound egotistic. Except that's what he was trying to do, especially with his global digests. And although his readership was small, each reader was a human being, each in his or her own small way having an effect on the world.

He thought about Wilmer Bracken. Mitch would need to call Miranda to see where she stood today with publishing the books.

At the office, he checked his phone messages. Miranda was ahead of him. An hour earlier she had left a message to call her.

"I read through both documents again over the weekend, reassuring myself about going forward," she told Mitch. "I'm even more convinced now that the public needs to be aware of his experience, and where the government has been going in both these areas."

"That's good to hear, Miranda."

"And this morning I started the processes of digitizing copy for eBooks, and getting type set for hard copies."

"Wow! Faith and action!"

"Precisely. Bina got a call from your guy in Boston. She likes and trusts him…as much I guess as a lawyer can like and trust another lawyer."

"Well, I sure like and trust him."

"Got it. Bina wants to meet with the author."

Mitch noticed how Miranda wasn't mentioning specific names, except for her own attorney. Reading the manuscripts probably had made her paranoid…or not…about her phone, or Mitch's, or both, being tapped.

"She wants to do this at her office. Can you have him there on Wednesday afternoon? Say 3:30? I'll email you the details."

"Send the email and I'll check with him tonight. Let you know tomorrow."

"That's good. Thank you, Mitch. Thanks for thinking of me and trusting me with this."

"I hope you'll thank me when the job's done."

"Mitch…"

"Yeah?"

"All is fundamentally well."

Mitch smiled. Miranda's pet summary after nearly every conversation they'd had over the years. Her way of saying the Higher Power is in charge.

"Yes. It is," he responded softly.

After a full Monday of editing articles and filling buckets, Mitch made his way to his Monday evening meeting on Sullivan Street.

As he sat listening to the speaker, someone was suddenly sitting next to him. It was Rachel. She looked stunning, even lovelier than when they had lived together.

They gazed at each other tentatively for a few seconds, then both turned to keep listening to the speaker.

After the meeting, she turned to him.

"Monica told me you saved my life."

"I think the doctors did that. And the Higher Power," Mitch said. He studied her. Then he smiled. "You clean up real well."

She gave a nervous laugh.

"I guess I did look like shit, didn't I?"

"Understatement."

"Yeah."

She looked around as if searching for what she needed to say next.

"You got time for coffee?" she asked. "Maybe we can talk?"

Mitch studied her clear, sad eyes.

"Rachel, I'm so grateful you're getting sober. But getting back together...you and I...that's not an option now."

"Is there...somebody else?"

"Well...yeah. But that's not the main point. You need to concentrate on getting back into the program full throttle. You know the deal."

The deal was to get back to real sobriety: begin again working with a sponsor, reviewing and again begin practicing the 12 Steps to living sober, and an honest relationship with a higher power, which would lead to honest relationships with everybody else. Rachel had done this before. He knew he didn't need to explain all of it to her.

She was fighting back crying. Mitch was suffering with her.

"Yeah. You're right. Well...thank you...for everything."

Mitch watched her. Then he gave her a firm but gentle hug. She hugged him firmly. He turned and moved toward the door. Monica had been standing there, watching it all from a distance.

Mitch paused, looking at her.

"She looks great, doesn't she?"

"She does," Monica said. "She misses you."

Mitch didn't respond, except for a gentle grasp of Monica's arm. Then he left.

As he walked to Wilmer Bracken's, Mitch continued what had become a habit: pausing every couple of blocks, looking around to see if anyone might be following him, either on the sidewalk or in a car. He didn't sense that tonight. In fact, he hadn't sensed it the entire weekend.

When Wilmer Bracken opened the door, he seemed to remember Mitch. He gave a nod and let Mitch enter.

As they sat on the couch, Mitch noticed the sound of soft orchestra music coming from Bracken's laptop on the dining table. Something like Mantovani, or Jackie Gleason's old albums.

"Wilmer, you're listening to some soft sounds there."

Bracken looked at him. Listened.

"Yeah. I remembered how I used to do that a lot. But I stopped, I guess, when my memory started slipping. I like it. It relaxes me."

Mitch watched him.

"I heard from the publisher today," Mitch said. "She's already started the process of setting type on your memoir, and the nuclear study."

Wilmer thought about that.

"Well…that's good. Isn't it."

"Yes. It's very good. Her attorney wants to meet with you at her office. On Wednesday afternoon at 3:30."

"Where is her office?"

Mitch gave a soft nervous laugh.

"Shit. I'm not sure. I've got so much going on, I forgot to look at the email. I'll find out and let you know."

"Are you going with me?"

"Yeah. I will."

"Okay."

Peggy Lee began "I'm in the Mood for Love".

"That's mighty romantic music," Mitch smiled.

"It's a station on Spotify."

"You remember that it's on Spotify?"

"Yes…I seem to be remembering more. I guess the medication is working."

"I guess it is," Mitch said in what could only be positive confusion. "Do you remember what you've done through today?"

Wilmer thought about it.

"Yes. Mostly. And I can remember some of yesterday."

Mitch was suddenly thinking how this was becoming a whole new ball game. If Wilmer was starting to remember more and more, would he eventually get to the point where he might begin reactivating his plan at mass murder?

Wilmer was looking off at nothing, listening to the music. Mitch decided he needed to think more how to address his concern with Wilmer's future intentions. He held off on questioning him tonight.

"Okay. I'm gonna go," Mitch said, standing up. "I'll come by here Wednesday about 2 pm. Then we can head to the publishing attorney's office."

"Those two officers came to see me," Wilmer said.

Mitch watched him.

"You mean from the CIA? Madison and Gonzalez?"

"Yes. You don't need to worry about them anymore. They won't bother you."

"Wilmer, that's what you told me about the other guy who was following me. What do you mean they won't bother me?"

"They wanted to know if I was going to publish anything about the CIA. I told them no. I told them they don't need to bother you anymore."

"And they believed you?"

Bracken thought about it. Then he looked at Mitch.

"It doesn't matter."

"Well…yeah, it does. If they don't believe you, won't they come back after me?"

"No. They won't. Somebody will come after me. But not you."

Mitch decided not to tell him that his view wasn't the same as Bena Saphire's or Stan Hadley's. He just nodded, gave a small wave, and headed to the door.

"Wednesday. Two o'clock," Bracken said to Mitch as he opened the door.

"Right. I'll see you then."

Wilmer Bracken had remembered.

Mitch met Rebel at 12 Chairs, the snug, glassed-in Israeli café on MacDougal.

"I've got us Mets tickets for Thursday night's game against Philly," Rebel informed him as she munched on her Pita Schnitzel. "You up for it?"

"Well…yeah. I thought you were going to Canada for your fashion shoot."

"My agent called. That's been delayed for at least a week. Some problem between the ad agency and the production company."

"Well, hooray for problems!" Mitch laughed, raising his hand in celebration, almost losing his tuna pita.

"Okay! Shall I book a car to drive us?"

"You've got the tickets," Mitch said. "I'll book the car. What time's the game?"

"Seven o'clock."

"Okay. I'll be over at your place and have the car pick us up there…when…six o'clock?"

"It's a date, Mr. Morgan!"

Mitch watched her as she jabbed her fork into her side salad.

"Rebel."

"Yeah?"

"Start writing."

She looked up at him. Cleared her throat.

"I do write. A little poetry."

"Really? I haven't seen you do that."

"When I'm with you, you're my poetry."

Suddenly Mitch felt warm all over.

"I'd like to read your poetry."

"Maybe. When I'm ready to show you."

"But you looked so happy just writing that paragraph for my blog. Don't you want to do some journalistic writing again?"

She chewed slowly, studying Mitch, then gazed past him at that space where we look for answers.

"Maybe."

"Are you afraid?"

"What makes you ask me that?"

"Well…I'm afraid before I write."

"You're not!" she almost yelled, catching herself, looking around to see if she disturbed other diners. She had, lightly. They both laughed. "Mitch, you write every day and night. You can't be afraid."

"Fear of the blank page, my dear. It's natural. But…at the same time, I'm also excited. Did you ever see the Broadway musical 'Sunday in the Park with George'?"

"No."

"It won the Pulitzer Prize for Drama. A Broadway musical! Anyway, at the end there's the scene where the actress on stage is reading from the protagonist's notebook. He's the French artist Georges Seurat. And she reads his words: 'White. A blank page or canvas. His favorite. So many possibilities.'"

Mitch felt tears starting to form in his eyes. Rebel was smiling at him.

"Anyway…that's why we feel both fear and excitement. So many possibilities at what we might put on the page."

"Yeah. I know that feeling," Rebel said.

They gazed lovingly at each other.

"So," Mitch said, "think about writing again."

"Okay. I'll think about it."

More gazing.

"Why don't you stay at my place tonight?" Mitch invited.

Now Rebel was tearing up. She nodded yes. Then she leaned over to whisper.

"I'd love to…but…Where are *you* gonna stay?"

Rebel marveled at how clean Mitch's apartment was, not knowing he had recently done his one and only spring cleaning.

"Yeah. I'm a stickler for the immaculate," Mitch quipped.

She strutted into his bedroom, felt the firmness of the futon, turned and fell onto it, holding up her arms.

"Come here and take me, lover!"

"Excuse me? Are you speaking to me?"

"Come here, you animal!"

Mitch went down on all fours. Then crawled across the floor to the futon in what had to be a Guinness speed record for human scooting.

Tuesday's deadline flowed smoothly until 4 p.m. Mitch received an unexpected email from Actors Equity Association. The union for actors on Broadway and stages nationwide was announcing the starting of negotiation on a new contract with the Broadway producers.

So Mitch needed to write a new front-page story. Usually he would have been ahead of the game on a major story for the industry. But now his attention was divided between the job and seeing Bracken published, and the effort alone of trying to keep it confidential was draining. And then there was Rebel, but time with her was consistently inspiring.

For the new story, he first reviewed Equity's press release, then typed up a headline, a lede summarizing the stories main points, and two more paragraphs. Then he quickly closed in italics with "This is a continuing story," a line telling the reader more would be coming.

Then he filed the article so it could immediately go onto the paper's website.

Next, he called Howard Lester, press liaison at The Broadway League, the trade association representing Broadway theater owners and producers.

"I was just fixing to call you!" Howard said, his eternal line whenever Mitch contacted him.

"I knew you were, Howard. I'm psychic." Mitch's eternal response.

"Mitch, I'm emailing…you…our announcement of the talks…right…now," Howard said as he evidently was just clicking his email's "send" button.

"You've got a quote from your boss?"

"The release indeed quotes Melanie Frazier, the league's president!"

"Between you and me, you foresee any problems ahead?"

"Not from our side. We believe the new contract we're proposing is not only fair, but generous!"

"Of course you do," Mitch smiled.

"As always!" said the chipper Lester.

That article completed at 5 pm, Mitch was able to file it, and watch the rest of deadline night fall into place. The team left before midnight.

The April night sky was clear for a change, with a comforting breeze. Traffic trailed steady down Broadway as Mitch walked home. As he crossed at West Fourth Street, Mitch moved through the NYU complex. When he reached the library across from

Washington Square Park, he suddenly stopped. Looked around to see if he might be followed. No one.

He thought of Wilmer Bracken's words. They won't come after Mitch. They'll come after him. He might be right.

THE MEETING

On Wednesday, Mitch took care of the basics at work. Then at noon, he stuck his head in to Abie Schulberg's office, telling her he was taking the afternoon off, but would return around 5 or 6 to check on the news.

After grabbing a tuna sub, Mitch headed south to Wilmer Bracken's. But before that, he had time to stop in at a couple of the myriad small, hole-in-the-wall galleries that inhabit the island's south. One basement wall was lined with novel watercolors, works of fantasy and humor. The second stop revealed large canvases of rich, thick, Impressionistic oils.

Mitch hadn't made such stops in a long while. His museum visits uptown recently with Rebel had reminded him how important art was to his spirit.

As Mitch approached Bracken's building, his smartphone hailed him.

"Mitch, It's Stan Hadley."

'Hey, Stan."

"I'm sorry I didn't contact you sooner. I'm going to join you at Bina Saphire's office for your 3:30 meeting."

"That's good!"

"Yeah. I should have given you an earlier heads up, but time got away from me."

"You're here in Manhattan now?"

"Yeah."

"Anything I need to know before the meeting."

"I don't think so. We'll know when we sit with your guy."

"Okay. See you soon."

Mitch clicked off, hanging on to Stan's phrase "your guy".

Wilmer Bracken is my guy, Mitch said to himself. That's right. A few months ago, they hadn't ever met. Now, he's my guy.

Mitch wondered what that actually meant. It meant he needed to protect Bracken as a confidential source until the books were out. But it also meant he had to protect himself, and everyone else, by keeping their relationship as secret as possible until then. But it seemed to be getting less possible. He thought to himself, we haven't got much time. Then he moved to his simple sober thinking: One day at a time. And today's Wednesday.

Mitch ordered an Uber for his and Bracken's trip uptown to Bina Saphire's office, which, happily was at the same location as Miranda's publishing company, but two floors up: the Flatiron Building. Mitch didn't know that until he had finally read Miranda's email.

In the car, Bracken remained quiet, watching lower Manhattan pass by. Then, as they neared their destination, Mitch spoke.

"You know, years ago when I first moved into Greenwich Village, I was so excited to be in the city, I constantly hit Broadway shows and the great museums up town. I was talking to a guy, who lived downtown a long time, telling him about my rambles. He said, 'You'll find a time when you'll never go above 14th Street.' I laughed. I thought he was full of it. But...damned if after about ten years...I found out he was right."

"You never go above 14th Street?"

"Only rarely, if my job requires it. But I do most of my work at the office, and interviews are mostly on the phone. I went up to the museums last weekend. But that's the first time in years. Strange."

Bracken looked at him, gave a slight smile and nodded.

Bina Saphire had pastry, coffee, tea, sparkling and regular water waiting on them when they arrived.

146

She sat behind her heavy oak desk topped with stacks of documents and a couple of open law books. Her guests sat in high-back green leather chairs in a semicircle in front of her: Miranda to her far right, Mitch next to her, then Bracken, then Stan Hadley to Bracken's right.

Saphire allowed brief introductions, and chatting about as long as two regular TV commercials. Then she got right to the point.

"Mr. Bracken," she said, and stopped there for about 10 long seconds, looking at Bracken, who watched her calmly. "You probably know you have the chance to send yourself and two other people in this room to prison. Maybe for a long time."

Bracken didn't speak. Or even nod. He just kept looking at Saphire as though she might be leading a meditation.

"How do you feel about that?" Saphire finally asked him.

Bracken looked at Mitch, then at Miranda, then back at Saphire.

"I don't feel about it."

"Excuse me?" Saphire responded. "It doesn't concern you that you might spend the rest of your life in jail?"

"No."

"That Ms. McCarthy here and Mr. Morgan might go to prison because of you?"

"No. I want the public to know what I've done, and what their government's done. Since both Ms. McCarthy and Mr. Morgan want the books published too, I take it that they agree with me."

"If I might ask a question," said Hadley, his huge body moving forward in his chair, looking at Bracken.

"Mr. Bracken, how can we be sure that the information in your memoir and the nuclear report are both...the truth?"

"It's the truth."

"How can we be sure?" Hadley repeated.

"Maybe you should ask Ms. McCarthy and Mr. Morgan why they're sure it's the truth. They're willing to get them both published."

"We do have a couple fact checkers reviewing the documents as we speak," Miranda said.

"After reading the memoir, I researched to verify if Mr. Bracken had actually mur…murdered Rebecca Sadler in Houston," Mitch said. "I found a news article about her dying in a house fire, as Mr. Bracken had stated in his memoir. He, of course, wasn't mentioned in the article. But I wanted to assure myself that she had actually existed, and had died. I was also able to verify dates for some of the Middle East activities he wrote about. I didn't know how to check on any specifics in the top-secret nuclear document. I found only general information online that some of the nuclear programs existed."

"I too checked and found articles on the Sadler death in Houston," Hadley said. "I found nothing about suspicion of murder."

"As you'd expect with a covert CIA operation," Saphire added. "Right, Mr. Bracken?"

Bracken calmly nodded.

"I've looked into Justice Department cases where they prosecuted agents who illegally revealed classified information," Saphire said. "I've no doubt, Mr. Bracken, they'll come after you."

Bracken simply watched her with no response.

"Stan?" she said, evidently asking Hadley if he agreed. He nodded yes.

"Stan and I agree that we can argue Constitutional protections for both Miranda and Mitch. There's plenty of legal precedent for that."

"That doesn't mean a jury or juries will agree with us," Hadley added. "But it's up to us to make a clear and solid argument of your protections under both freedom of the press and freedom of expression, and the legal precedents Bina alluded to. We'll dedicate ourselves to that."

"Do you have any legal counsel, Mr. Bracken?" Saphire asked.

Bracken shook his head no.

"I suggest you find some," Saphire said.

Bracken didn't respond.

"Miranda, I believe you want to speak to Mr. Bracken about publishing the two documents."

The publisher opened a manila folder she was holding.

"Mr. Bracken, first let me make clear that we're a small publisher. Our books have traditionally been romantic fiction for a primarily female audience. So, delving into nonfiction, and particularly into your covert, lethal reality, is a first for us."

Bracken didn't respond, only watched her.

"Because we're a small publisher, we're always on a tight budget. Very, very rarely have we offered a lucrative contract to an author. And rarely have provided an advance. But we're prepared to offer you an advance of..."

"I don't want one," Bracken said flatly.

"Excuse me?" Miranda countered.

"I don't want an advance. Use that money for publishing. Or for getting the word out...marketing."

Silence. Miranda and Saphire looked at each other.

"Well," Miranda said. "In that case, let me move forward and tell you we're willing to offer you a contract for..."

"I don't want any money," Bracken said, his voice direct and sincere.

"Mr. Bracken..."

"I don't want any money. I don't need money. The government has given me a retirement that's more than I need. I've got a health insurance policy that's probably better than the president's. I have what I need."

"Mr. Bracken," said Saphire, "I'm not sure how the law reads on this, or how the Justice Department has treated it in the past. But have you considered that they might void your future retirement, and your insurance?"

"Let 'em try."

Silence.

Saphire looked at Miranda, who seemed at a loss. She looked at Hadley, who gave a shrug. She reached out to Miranda who leaned forward and handed her the folder with the contract. She opened it, took a pen, and began marking on the typed contract.

"So," said Saphire, "I can amend this contract stating the publisher will publish both books…with no monetary payment due to you now or in the future?"

Bracken nodded.

"That means you agree with what I just said?"

Bracken nodded.

"Mr. Bracken, could you please give me a vocal response, so we all know what you mean."

"Yes," Bracken said. "I agree with what you just said. I'll receive no payment."

"Thank you." Saphire watched him. Then: "Well, Miranda, shall we move ahead with the publishing process, understanding that Mr. Bracken has refused any monetary payment for the two books…" She looked at Bracken. "…including royalties?"

Bracken nodded. "Yes. Including royalties."

Saphire marked on the contract. When finished, she rose, walked to and out the door to her secretary's desk, handing her the contract and speaking to her. The secretary immediately began making the changes to the document on her computer.

Saphire returned, sat, and gazed at Bracken.

"Still, Mr. Bracken," Saphire added, "we hope you will be willing to consult with the publisher as they may need your confirmation or advice on information within the two books?"

"Sure," Bracken said.

"Well," said Saphire, breathing in deeply, "if there's nothing else…"

"I…I've got a question," Mitch said, and he looked at Bracken. "Wilmer, I want to ask this in front of the two attorneys, because it might affect all of us legally."

Mitch let out a breath, thinking of how to formulate the question. Then:

"You state in your memoir you were planning a mass execution of people at the World Economic Forum. You recall that?"

Bracken watched Mitch, blinking his eyes, seeming to try and remember. Then:

"Yeah…yeah…I remember that."

"I believed that, with your loss of memory, your plan had been abandoned. Now you've indicated to me that, with your new medication, your memory is slowly returning."

Bracken continued to watch him with no response.

"My question is…are you again considering following through on that lethal plan?"

Dead silence.

Wilmer watched Mitch. Then he frowned as if either trying to remember, or trying to decide.

"I don't think I'll live long enough even if I wanted to try it."

"What do you mean?" Mitch asked.

"They'll come after me as soon as the books are out."

"Do you mean, you believe they'll kill you?" Hadley asked.

Bracken nodded.

Dead silence.

"Let me ask you," Bracken said, looking at Saphire, "in your research of these legal cases…did you find any CIA officer who revealed material as serious and deep as what I'm revealing?"

Saphire watched him. Then she looked at Hadley. They both looked at Bracken. They shook their heads no.

"You'll need to get your legal counsel to look at that," Saphire said.

Bracken didn't respond.

Mitch wasn't satisfied.

"Wilmer, I'm still not clear on your answer to my question."

Bracken stared at him.

"What was your question again?"

"Will you follow through on your plan of a mass execution at the World Economic Forum…if the CIA doesn't kill you? Or before the government might imprison you?"

Bracken stared at him with a strange calm, considering the question.

"No," he finally said. "I don't feel like that anymore."

All watched him. He leaned back in his chair and said no more.

The secretary entered with copies of the amended contract, handing them to Saphire. She gave the pact a once over and seemed satisfied.

"Mr. Bracken, will you and Miranda please read the contract now. If you're satisfied with it, please sign it."

Before she could stand to take the contract to them, Bracken had risen and moved to her desk, reaching out for the document. That led Miranda to do the same.

Bracken took the document.

"Do you have a pen?" he asked.

Saphire handed him one. He took it and signed the contract without even reading it.

Silence as everyone watched him. Then Saphire.

"Miranda, could you please read and sign it."

Miranda took the document, asking Saphire, "Where did you make changes?"

"Here…and here," Saphire said, pointing to specific paragraphs.

Then Miranda signed it.

A long silence. Then Saphire:

"Okay. Mr. Bracken, I strongly suggest you find legal counsel immediately. And could you please leave contact information with Miranda in case she or her staff have any questions about the documents?"

"I'll only talk to her or Mr. Morgan," said Bracken, staring at Saphire. Then he turned and walked to the door as if to say this meeting is over.

And it was.

Then, at the door, Bracken turned and looked at them.

"Thank you…all," he said, and walked out.

Mitch rose, looked at Miranda, who gave him an ironic smirk and little farewell wave of the hand. He looked at Hadley, who winked at him, nodding toward Saphire, a sign he was going to stay and talk. He looked at Saphire who was staring at him, studying him.

"Bye," Mitch said softly, following Bracken out of the office.

Bracken was silent on the ride back downtown. Mitch didn't know if he was angry, or simply watching the passersby and buildings. Then:

"They're good people, aren't they?" Bracken said.

"You mean at our meeting?"

Bracken nodded.

"Yes," Mitch said. "They're brilliant people with good hearts."

Mitch studied him as he looked out the window.

"Wilmer, what are you going to do about getting an attorney to represent you?"

"I'll take care of that."

"Do you want me to…"

"I'll take care of it."

"Okay."

The car pulled up in front of the *Center Stage* offices. Mitch started to get out.

"Wilmer, I'll check back with you tomorrow."

He turned and looked in at Bracken, who was watching him.

"It was a good day," Bracken said, his face looking peaceful.

"Yes. I guess so. See you."

At his desk, Mitch checked his phone messages. Both Miranda and Stan had left voicemails to call them.

"He's a dangerous guy," Stan said.

"Well...yeah...that's a given."

"I don't mean from reading about his past. I mean from my sitting there and watching him. He's a psychopath."

"Yeah...well...I've heard that term, Stan, but I'm not sure specifically what that means."

"I watch him and I see this impaired empathy and remorse. But he's not uninhibited like a psychopath. He's goddam cold and calculating."

"Maybe it's just him struggling to get his memory functioning again."

"I knew a couple of guys in the NFL that were like him. They'd just as soon rip your head off and eat your brains, and never consider that insane. And now and then I meet with a prisoner who's up for parole to see if I want to represent him. When I see this in him, I say no way."

Mitch was quiet, considering Stan's appraisal.

"So, what are you saying? Are you saying let's get away from him? Not publish the books?"

"I don't know yet. Let me think about it. I'll call you tomorrow. In the meantime, watch yourself."

"Well...thanks for that. After I've spent hours alone with the guy."

"But his memory's coming back. We don't know what that means...what he'll do."

Silence. Then Mitch:

"Okay. I'll watch myself. Thanks for being there today. You helped."

"You too. You got to the lethal question we were all thinking. I should have asked that. Not you."

"Ah, you're just a coldblooded lawyer, Hadley. I'm a crusty, mean, aggressive journalist."

"Bye."

"Bye."

Mitch called Miranda.

"Mitch, I don't know what to think about this guy. I've never met anybody before like him. I've never met an author who didn't want to get paid. It's like it's a conscience thing with him. A way of public confession. Yet when he sits there and looks at you...he's...he's..."

"He's a killer, Miranda. He's a government-trained killer. Who also happens to be intelligent and aware. Or as much as he can be while he struggles with his memory. When he had all his faculties...I can see now why he moved to all these different assignments. He was like an intelligence man for all seasons."

"Do you think he'd follow through on his plan, if he were able? Or was he telling us the truth?"

"I don't have an answer. But I'm paying very close attention."

"Be careful. Okay?"

"Faith and action. All is fundamentally well."

"Maybe." She'd never said that before.

"Miranda, Wilmer Bracken saved my life. He also helped me save Rachel's life. We got her out of a drug den."

"Really?"

"He pulverized a guy who was about to stab me. He could have killed him. But he didn't."

Silence.

"After that...after we got Rachel to the hospital and doctors saved her...after all that...you know what he said to me?"

"What?"

"'It was a good night.' That was his summary. When I left him today after our meeting, you know what he said? 'It was a good day.'"

"He said that?"

"That's all he said about it. Oh, actually, earlier he said, 'They're good people, aren't they.'"

He heard Miranda let out a deep sigh.

"Okay. Let's get these damn things published and break some glass. Bye."

"Miranda…you have any idea when they might be out?"

"I'm shooting for two weeks. That's an emergency rush just to get them online and in print. No way to distribute them by then, or get reviews, much less market them."

"But at least they'll be out? Made public."

"Yes."

"You're wonderful."

"Bye."

He hadn't given her Stan's analysis. He figured Stan had already shared that with her and Bina Saphire.

Mitch and Rebel's sweating bodies lay pressed against each other, both struggling to breathe.

"My…god…" Rebel whispered. "I thought you were going to rip both me and the mattress off its frame and fly us to heaven. What's got into you?"

Mitch was quiet. Then…

"It was a good day." Then he gave a slight laugh.

Rebel looked at him. "What's going on?"

He looked at her and smiled.

"I've decided I really like you," he said softly.

She grinned.

"You sure do!"

She started pressing kisses all over his face.

"Hey! You! Stop this wicked assault!"

"Never!"

She finally did. They both were laughing, holding each other in that precious way that rises when two people realize how they've survived the vulnerability of chancing love.

THE CONFESSION

Thursday morning, Mitch walked out into the April day, felt the cold wind, looked at the cloudy sky, and went back in and grabbed a heavier jacket and Irish country hat.

At work, he managed to get an impromptu phone interview with Joseph Cohen, president of Actors Equity. The respected performer was more than ready to discuss his response to the article on the producers' contract proposal, and his view of what the stage actors needed for a reasonable agreement.

During the interview, Mitch's mind wandered a couple of times, thinking of Rebel. When he hung up from the interview, he smiled, remembering that he and she would attend the Mets game that night.

An hour later, as he finished up the Equity article, his smartphone rang. He saw it was Rebel.

"Is this the world's most beautiful human?" Mitch said when answering.

"Mitchell...what the fuck is going on?"

Her voice was shaky.

"What's the matter?"

"A guy knocked on my door a while ago. He said he was with the CIA. He started asking me questions about you?"

"What!"

"What the...fuck...is going on!"

"Where are you?"

"I'm at home."

"Can you meet me in Washington Square Park? Say 15 minutes?"

Silence. Then a weak "Okay."

The two sat on a green bench in a corner of the park. Rebel was wearing a leather jacket of creamy green and a matching beret to protect her from the chilling breeze. Mitch held her hand. It was cold and trembling. But she seemed more angry than afraid.

There hadn't been a kiss or hello. Only "What the fuck is going on?"

"Did this guy have an ID?" Mitch asked.

"Yes."

"Did you let him in?"

"Fuck no I didn't let him in!"

"What did you tell him?"

"I didn't tell him shit! I said you were a journalist, and if he had any questions about you, he needed to ask you."

"Good. That's good. Did he offer any information? About why he was there."

"I think he was trying to scare me into talking. He said that three CIA officers had been in contact with you. And all three had disappeared. He made it sound like you might have killed them."

Mitch's body grew hot then cold. What had Bracken done?

"He's full of shit! Rebel, I'm so sorry…"

"Mitchell…what the fuck is going on?"

Her green eyes bored through him.

Silence. Then:

"I can't tell you what's going on. The less you know, the better for you legally. I can tell you I'm a journalist protecting a confidential source."

"The CIA's after an actor?"

"No."

She gazed at him, her eyes pleading.

"I wish I could tell you more. Actually, I hope to be able to tell you in a couple of weeks. When the book's out."

"You've written a book?"

"No…I've helped get one published. But that's all I can tell you now. Please wait two weeks. It will all be clear then."

She watched him, huffed out in desperation, and wrapped her arms around him.

"Please tell me you're not in danger."

He skirted.

"Actually, I'm just doing what journalists do worldwide. Protecting a source."

Her hold on him seemed to soften with that. But she still held him tight. And he her.

A sudden heavier wind swept in. And just as suddenly snow began to fall. One of those Manhattan April days when the gods had decided winter wasn't over.

"Come on," Mitch said. "Let's get somewhere warm."

As they walked, their arms around each other, Mitch looked at the sky.

"I guess the Mets game is off."

"Probably just as well," Rebel said in a tired whisper. "You need to get back to work."

"What are you going to do?"

She looked at him. Her eyes were weary but warm.

"What does every woman do after being confronted by the CIA? I'm fucking going shopping."

They both released a frustrated laugh. They kissed, then hugged each other as they walked on.

As they moved past the NYU business school, she told him to take care of himself. She told him again as they turned the corner on

Broadway. She decided she would walk up to the Strand bookstore. And as she left him, she told him again.

Each time he said he would. Inside he hoped he could.

Mitch hit his regular after-work meeting, got some spiritual stamina, then headed to confront Wilmer Bracken.

At Bracken's apartment, Mitch stood glaring at the former agent, who was sitting on the couch. Afraid and angry, Mitch had prayed for guidance as he had knocked on Bracken's door. It didn't help much. Inside, he related Rebel's story about the CIA agent and how it had frightened her.

Bracken had listened calmly, silently. When Mitch had finished, Bracken opened his small notebook and began writing in it. After about 15 seconds, he looked up at Mitch.

"What was the agent's name?" Bracken asked.

"I don't know what his fucking name was! But I want to know what he wanted to know: What happened to those three CIA agents?"

"You don't need to know."

"Listen! They came after my girlfriend! I'm mad as hell about that! And I'm afraid!"

Bracken watched him, an expression of what seemed to be quiet, calm analysis.

"Bracken, what the hell happened to those…"

"You don't need to know."

"They came after my girl. They'll come back after me! I need to…"

"No, you don't!" Bracken glared back, then calmed. "They're not after you. They're after me. They'll be coming soon. After me. If they do come back to talk with you, you won't know anything to tell them."

"The guy practically accused me of killing them!"

Bracken flipped a few pages back through his notebook, read quickly, then looked at Mitch.

"How much do you know about those three agents?"

"What do you mean?"

"If I came and asked you what you actually know...about those three agents...what would you tell me about them?"

"Well...I saw the first guy by my office building and I grew suspicious. Later that day at lunch, I saw him across the street and took a quick photo of him with my smartphone. I saw him later that same day in Washington Square Park, took another photo of him. He saw that, turned and hurried away. I tried to follow him, but he had disappeared. I met with you, showed you his photo. And I never saw him again."

Bracken had listened, not writing.

"Good," Bracken said, as if Mitch had just given him news about the weather. "What about the other two?"

"They knocked on my door one night, showed me a picture of you, and asked if I knew you. I didn't say if I did or didn't. I turned the tables on them, got my notebook and started to try and interview them. They immediately turned and left. One said they'd be back."

Bracken gave a slight laugh.

"Did they come back?"

"No. One left a business card in my door. I...I told you about them. But I never saw them again."

"Did I kill them?"

"Hell, I don't know!"

"That's right. You don't know. Do you know anything else about the three?"

"No."

"That's right. So if someone comes to talk to you about them...You tell them what you just told me. You don't really know anything. Except you told me about them and never saw them again."

"What if they don't believe me?"

"It's their job to know if someone is lying or not. And it's their job to lie, to manipulate you to find out the truth."

"My girlfriend said she thought the agent was lying to her to manipulate her."

"Yes."

Bracken reached in his right pants pocket, pulled out his keyring, and took a key off of it. He reached out to Mitch.

"Here."

"What's this?"

"It's an extra key to my apartment. In case you need to get in."

"Why would I need to get in if you're not here?"

"You may need to. After they come after me."

They watched each other. Mitch breathed a nearly inaudible "Fuck." He took the key.

"So…you think they'll arrest you…or try to kill you?"

"I'll try to make sure neither happens."

A steady snow was falling as Mitch trudged his way to Rebel's. His paranoia was hawking him, so he'd stop every block, looking around for any sinister stalker. No one he could see.

Inside the warmth of Rebel's apartment, he sat at the dining table, looking in at her in the kitchen. She was chopping carrots with vigor, as if they might be fingers of a CIA agent.

"You need any help?" he asked.

"No, this is the last of the assault," she said, indicating she might have been disposing of the imaginary enemy.

She emptied the carrots into the salad bowl, mixing them in with the other veggies. Then she brought it into the table.

"If you would, please, for our salad plates?"

She paused, looked down at Mitch. He was intensely staring at her. She saw he was on edge. She smiled, bent down, and gently kissed his lips.

"You're my hero, you know that," she whispered to him.

He smiled meekly, and let out a long breath.

She did a small dance back to the stove, took the soup pan and poured the steaming contents into two soup bowls on the counter. She brought one in and put it in front of Mitch.

He breathed in the floating steam.

"Mmmm. This smells like New Orleans."

"You are now in the Vieux Carre, cher," she smiled, walking in with her bowl and sitting just around the table corner from him.

"Shrimp bisque?"

"Shrimp, crab, and corn bisque. Made with love. For the man sitting next to me."

Mitch looked out the window at the snowy night.

"Perfect night for it," he said softly. Then he looked at Rebel. Reached over and gently touched her cheek.

She smiled, took his hand, kissed it, and gave it back to him.

"Eat it while it's hot, babe."

Silence as they sat eating. Then:

"Rebel...I'm so sorry about what happened to you today."

"You know...I've thought about it. It wasn't that much really. I was scared for a little while as I spoke with him, then got mad actually. And he could see I had nothing to tell him. Then he was gone. But then I became afraid for you. Mitchell, I'm sorry I snapped at you like I did..."

"You had a right to. I wish I could talk to you about this. I'll be able to soon."

"I'm proud of you for protecting your source. I know it has to be hard for you."

They looked at each other with a deep sensitivity.

"I talked to the source," Mitch said. "I was told we don't have to worry. They're not after you and me."

"Do you believe him?"

"I don't believe I said it's a him."

"Oh…well…do you believe what you were told?"

"Yes."

He smiled at her.

"And I believe that, if you're proud of me now…you'll be very proud when you read the book."

Rebel gazed at him, started to cry, got up and pushed herself into his lap, wrapping her arms around him and looking in his eyes. She kissed him. They hugged each other. Held each other in silence. Then:

"Mitchell…"

"Yes."

"The bisque is getting cold."

"But we're not."

She laughed softly. They held each other tighter.

THE OFFER

The snow had continued through the night, so it was a slow walk to work Friday. At his desk, Mitch decided to check on any possible update with Equity and the Broadway producers on their new contract negotiations, which had started Thursday. The word was they had received and reviewed each other's contract proposal document, and today would start discussions. Mitch wrote the brief update and placed it on the *Center Stage* website.

He decided to call Miranda.

"We're moving quickly," she said. "Our fact checkers are making good progress. They've been able to verify dates and outcomes of some of his listed activities. But there are also a lot of covert activities they have no way of finding online, including government and major news and investigative sites. So we'll have to take his word for it."

"That's good, isn't it? Fresh news, so to speak?"

"Yeah. And it should be good for marketing, including creating an air of mystery that should attract readers."

"And maybe film producers."

"Maybe. The way we're going, I think we might have the ebook ready early next week. Same with the nuclear report."

"Will you publish those before the print editions?"

"We'll see. We may have to, just to make sure we get something to the public before anyone tries to shut us down."

"What happens if you get shut down."

"I've got a plan."

Since she didn't say specifically what, Mitch didn't ask.

"Now, two long-range points I want to talk to you about," Miranda said. "First, Bina suggested this and I readily agreed. We're forming a new corporation for handling this. A new publishing company that will start with the memoir and report. I've decided to call it Soule Books, s-o-u-l-e. We're naming it in honor of Captain Silas Soule, the U.S. Army's first whistleblower. He refused the order to join the murder of Indian women, children, and elderly men at the Sand Creek Massacre in 1864. We'll want to publish books by whistleblowers in business and government worldwide. Bina is filing the paperwork today."

"Miranda...that's amazing! And you're moving at jet speed."

"I've been wanting to do something of service in publishing for a while now. Just couldn't get specific. What you brought us made it specific, and something I can really be dedicated to. Bina liked the idea because it can help society, and also may take legal pressure off of Heartfelt Books when the government comes after us."

Mitch was feeling a deep warmth. He had loved and admired his dear friend for years. Now both those feelings were in full force.

"Miranda, I hope you get a Nobel for that! You'll deserve one."

"I just hope we can get these two books out without getting raided. But let me get to my second point.

"You brought these books to us. You immediately saw their value, and the need to reveal them to the public. I've seen your online global digests. You have a good grasp of world affairs, a good conscience, and a deep journalistic background. I'd like for you to be our editor-in-chief for this new company."

Silence. Mitch was stunned. Miranda gave a soft laugh.

"You don't have to answer right away, Mitch."

"Miranda, I don't know. I'm not a book editor."

"You won't be editing the books. You'll be overseeing the editors for accuracy. And you'll be making the editorial decisions about what books we should purchase. Actually, you'll be reporting and working with me on those decisions, but you'll be doing the day-to-day supervision. You'll be good at it. You obviously know how to talk to a whistleblower, and can get him or her to cooperate. Plus, I'll be next door to confer with you on the everyday functions."

"Bina said you might lose all profits in lawsuits. I hate to be materialistic, but If there's no money, there's no salary, and I can end up homeless."

"I'm working on that now. You'll have money. You let me know how much you need to make the move, and we'll work it out. Faith and action, Mitch!"

"Faith and action," Mitch repeated weakly. "Let me think about it over the weekend. I've gotta process through my ego-centered fear."

"Well, you know where to take that."

"Yep. Upstairs. But it does sound damn exciting if we can pull it off."

"I like that you said 'we'. Mitch, we've known each other a long time. We care about each other, and we're of like minds on how we need to live both spiritually and professionally. Who knows, maybe WE'll win a Nobel!"

"You're quite a recruiter, Miranda."

"Let me know. Oh!!"

"What?"

"One other important thing we need from you by Monday: two forewords, one for the memoir and another for the nuclear report. They don't have to be long. Just a clear explanation of how you came on the material for the two books, and why you brought them to Soule Books. Okay?"

Mitch gave a deep sigh.

"Yeah. Okay. Monday."

"Hey."

"What."

"Go, team!" she quipped with a slight laugh. Mitch laughed softly. They hung up.

Later that morning, Stan Hadley called. He said he had dedicated himself fully to supporting the publishing of the two books. "I'll be honored to be your attorney wherever this takes us," Hadley said. "What do you hear?"

"All seems to be going well uptown. E-books may be ready early next week. Miranda has decided to start a new publishing company to print and sell books by whistleblowers nationwide. Bina's filing the corporate paperwork. Miranda wants me to be editor in chief."

"Really!"

"Yeah."

"You gonna do it?"

"I told her I'd decide this weekend."

"Do it!"

"Maybe. Probably."

"What do you hear from your guy?"

"He expects they'll be on him soon. He didn't say when, but I figure for sure after publication. Probably immediately."

"Makes sense. How's his temperament?"

"He seems to be remembering more, leading him to think logically about the future. The near future anyway. He seems aware but not worried."

"Understandable, considering his history."

"Yeah."

After lunch, Mitch was writing a column overviewing possibilities in the new Broadway actors-producers contract. He could update it after talking to both sides at deadline Tuesday.

His smartphone perked up. It was Rebel.

"My agent just called. I'm heading upstate for the L.L. Bean shoot."

"I thought you were going to Canada."

169

"The ad agency and production company had a falling out. Now, with this blizzard that's come through, the new production company's going to shoot upstate."

"When do you leave?"

"In about an hour."

"Whoa! Faster than a speeding bullet!"

"Yeah. I'm taking Amtrak. That way I avoid any highway or traffic problems."

"Rebel, where are you going specifically?"

"Lake Placid. We've got reservations at the Lake Placid Lodge. "Luxurious and rustic," my agent says. I guess he felt he needed to convince me to go immediately."

Mitch could feel her grinning over the phone.

"Will you let me know you got there okay?"

"What…do I owe you money?"

"Ha ha," he faked. "I love all of you. Even your sarcasm."

"Back at you, handsome. Talk later."

"Hey! How long will you be gone?"

"Over the weekend for sure. Maybe a little longer if any problems creep in."

So suddenly Mitch's Friday night had been robbed of romance. He felt very lonely. But he knew a meeting would help.

After his regular meeting he grabbed a quick dinner with his sponsee, got caught up, and headed to his apartment. This would be a good night to update his *Global Tech & Surveillance* digest.

In the midst of his curating, his smartphone awoke. It was a text from Wilmer Bracken:

Any luck at the bookstore today?

His CIA covert instincts were still alert, thought Mitch.

They told me my order should be in early next week. I'll let you know.

Sounds good.

Mitch was concentrating his digest on surveillance. His lead article covered the near-fascist Congress passing, and the approaching-fascist President signing, a new federal law requiring the nation's contractors and landlords to build surveillance cameras into all new construction, both business and residential. The camera firms were required to connect their technology to each local government's police force.

Businesses were required to run the security cameras 24/7. Homeowners and renters of homes and apartments would have the option of turning the tech off when home, but were required to turn it on when leaving.

The stated rationale was to fight crime through recording any illegal intrusion into the premises. But in his blog, Mitch would stress the dangers to privacy, considering the intricacy and power of technology to intrude on every aspect of life.

He pointed out how tech had become so refined over the past decade with Artificial Intelligence, connecting all systems from smartphone to PC to laptop to mainframe to satellite, that governments globally were able to even surveil one another, and surveil that surveillance.

He wrote of the article placed in the digest about New York City's Police Department forming a drone unit: a massive operation which would cover the boroughs with drones the size of sparrows. They would patrol city streets, alleyways, parking lots and parking decks, virtually unnoticed by citizens. Combining this with the city's legion of public security cameras meant crooks couldn't hide in public, but neither could regular folks. And the technology was so refined it could literally record any conversation of anyone outdoors.

Now he could foresee tech completely infiltrating American citizens' homes. Big Brother had been perfected in other authoritarian countries ranging from China, Russia, and India to dictatorships on every continent, including some EU members.

Only the smaller Scandinavian countries had developed citizen countermeasures to hold off the onslaught. Their smaller, well-educated populations had solidified activism with technology.

171

Activist organizations in Norway and Sweden had built technology departments. Their nerds had developed apps distributed to citizens for their smartphones. Through those, the activists could communicate instantly to citizens about proposed regulations or laws endangering privacy. And the apps could allow citizens to register to vote, and also connect them instantly to their legislators to voice their opposition or favor to proposed legislation or any government activity. The sheer numbers bombarding a legislator was a message that he or she or they would not be in office long if they went against their constituents.

Larger governments had been able to censor such technology as well as the flow of the Internet. And America was settling in as a mainstay of that. Mitch saw this new legislation as a curse, solidifying censorship and repression.

It was a little after midnight when he had finished his written and video blog and placed the digest online. He was tired. He flopped down on his living-room couch, breathed deep, and soaked in Massanet's "Meditation" flowing from his PC's speaker. And he slept.

He was roused by his smartphone.

"I'm here." Rebel's voice messaged weariness.

"Mmm," groaned Mitch.

"I wake you?"

"Mmm."

"Well…you told me to let you know when I got here."

"What time is it?"

"6:35, Eastern."

"You safe and okay?"

"Yes. Mitchell…"

"Mmm."

"I miss you."

"I'll miss you when I wake up."

"You don't miss me in your sleep?"

"Mmm."

"Okay, I get it. Go back to dreamland. Gimme a call when you're conscious."

"Mmm."

Mitch dragged in to his futon, falling onto it like a skydiver into a cloud.

THE CONFLICT

Beethoven's Fifth urged Mitch awake. It was 10:25 Saturday morning. He deep breathed his way into reviewing the 12 Steps and praying for conscious contact. Then he got up and showered.

Now dressed, he plopped on the couch, and called Rebel. Her soft voice acknowledged her voicemail. She was probably out on the shoot. He envisioned her in a warm, snappy L.L. Bean winter coat, her face rosy-cold and beautiful. He smiled, sighed, got up and headed out to grab some brunch, landing at the Quantum Leap around the corner.

At his window seat, he gazed out at the passersby negotiating the slick sidewalks as he relished his omelet and gluten-free berry and banana pancakes.

Then he overheard two NYU students a table over.

"How the hell did it start?"

"It seems both Russia and the U.S. claim possession of a fresh lake and also lands containing rare-earth minerals in the Arctic. Firefights broke out at both places. Then planes came in, bombing."

Mitch turned. He saw one of the students was reading *The New York Times*.

"Shit!" yelped the reader.

"What?"

"The article says down here that the U.S. and China navies also got into a firefight in the South China Sea. Just a couple of hours later. The U.N.'s called an emergency Security Council meeting for Sunday."

Mitch paid his bill and slid back to his apartment. On his way, he stopped briefly at Grace's shop to grab some herbal tea.

He was at his PC and also checking the TV reports.

"The UN Security Council is scheduled to meet at 10 am Sunday, and will try to bring calm to the growing conflicts," CNN's broadcaster was saying.

Mitch immediately thought of Wilmer Bracken. He had planned a mass execution at the full World Economic Forum meeting in January. With his memory slowly returning, would he want to take on the UN?

Mitch thought about it. No, he didn't think Wilmer would consider acting on just a body of politicians, even the President. His writing indicated he wanted the world's major moneychangers and techsters. Mitch breathed out in relief.

He sipped his herbal tea, and moved from his PC to his couch to watch TV.

He began considering how these not-so-sudden acts of violence might evolve into larger conflict. With these major combatants all being members of the UN Security Council, could that body come to any agreement? Or would the violence spiral?

He thought about Kenneth T., the retired special forces fellow. He had said he could feel war coming. He appeared to be right.

Mitch had written in past blogs about both the Arctic and the South China Sea. How ice in the former was melting rapidly due to climate change, allowing access to the vast area's oil, minerals, and precious fresh water; and the various countries that bordered and claimed territory there. In the latter, how protective China was of the South China Sea, and how the U.S. for years had challenged Beijing by running naval vessels through those waters.

Sooner or later, both those dangerous areas had to erupt in conflict. Now it had happened on the same day.

Then the CNN broadcaster grabbed Mitch.

"We've just got a special report from Blake Simmons in Lake Placid, New York. Come in Blake."

Lake Placid? Rebel! What's this!?!

The picture segued to a handsome broadcaster standing lakeside, surrounded by a landscape of snow.

"The Bilderberg Group was founded in 1954 with the original purpose to prevent another world war. It brought together top financial and political people from Europe and North America who met in a private, off-the-record setting. So they could speak freely without press coverage. It worked so well, they decided to meet yearly."

Simmons slowly took a few steps and did an about face. The camera followed him, revealing behind him a large, two-story building of old stone and balconies.

"This is the historic Lake Placid Lodge. A centerpiece of activity for past billionaires like the Carnegies, Rockefellers, and Vanderbilts. And today, we've received word of a scheduled emergency meeting here...called for a select number of the Bilderberg Group.

"Usually about 150 VIPs gather in mid-May for the private Bilderberg meeting. But on Monday, some 50 of its number will gather here to discuss the growing emergency situation involving Russia, China, and the United States.

"Our source says that the elite crowd will include chairmen of America's largest banks, technology firms, and weapons manufacturers. They'll try to get a handle on how to quell what could turn into a treacherous global conflict. Political leaders will also join them at meetings on Monday. And we understand the President will come here following her Security Council meeting at the UN on Sunday..."

Mitch was breathing heavily. He was feeling suddenly overwhelmed by double trouble. Rebel was staying at the lodge. Would she get caught up in all this? And what would this mean to Wilmer Bracken?

Mitch jumped from the couch to his desk, took out his keyring, found his desk key and unlocked the bottom drawer. He pulled out

Bracken's memoir, quickly thumbing through it to one specific page. He re-read it:

I saw that in nine months, the World Economic Forum would be meeting in Davos, Switzerland. The gathering would include the world's powerbrokers: the billionaire bankers and industrialists, the billionaire techsters, and the world's leading politicians and elected officials. They were the manipulators and profiteers of Endless War.

They would be in one location. The meeting area would be vast. But my training and experience in logistics and drone attacks would serve me well in this mass execution.

"Holy fuck!"

Mitch's mind flashed with multiple visions of disaster. The leading powerbrokers Bracken had listed as his desired victims would now be at Lake Placid. The top American bankers, techsters, politicians, and now also the weapons magnates. And in a smaller location. This would be a prime target for Bracken. IF he believed he could pull it off. And IF he wanted to.

What did he say in that meeting at Bena Saphire's office? Mitch had asked him if he still planned that mass execution.

"No," Bracken had said. "I don't feel like that anymore."

Then Mitch recalled how Bracken had told him that CIA agents lie. Could he have been lying?

Mitch grabbed his smartphone and texted Bracken:

Are you in?

He waited. No immediate response. He'd call Rebel and check back on Bracken.

He got Rebel's voicemail again.

He checked back on the text. Nothing from Bracken.

He clicked on to his Uber app. The sidewalks were slick, but city plows had done a good job clearing the streets. He would ride rather than walk to Bracken's.

Mitch knocked on Bracken's door.

No answer. He knocked again.

No answer. He tried the door handle. Locked.

He breathed a brief prayer for guidance. He reached in his pocket, pulled out his keyring, grabbed Bracken's key and unlocked the door. He slowly opened it.

"Wilmer! It's Mitchell Morgan!...Wilmer!?!"

No answer.

He looked in. The curtains were closed, making the room semi-dark. He stepped inside, listening. No sound. He stepped to the dining table. No laptop. He didn't see it in the living room.

He stepped into the bathroom. No one there.

Maybe he took his laptop and went out to eat.

Or maybe they came and got him.

Mitch stepped back to the dining table, his eyes more focused now in the dim light. He looked down. There on the table lay a piece of torn scratch paper.

"Oh...fuck!"

In what looked like a hurried scrawl were written three words:

Lake Placid Lodge

The Bilderbergs were meeting on Monday. This was Saturday afternoon. That would give Bracken a day to get there, a day to set up and execute...literally.

Whatever was going on, he needed to contact Rebel. To tell her to get out of there.

He called her phone. Her voicemail again. He decided to leave her a message.

"Rebel. You need to get away from the Lake Placid Lodge. I can't explain now, but everyone there may be in danger. I'm not kidding. Get out of there as soon as you can."

He checked his text. He hadn't heard from Bracken. He called his smartphone number for the first time.

No answer. No voicemail to leave a message. But the smartphone would record Mitch's phone number. Maybe Bracken would call back. But maybe not. Mitch couldn't wait to see.

As Mitch made his way back home, he tried to envision what Bracken would use if he had decided to act. He had written about drones. But where would he get a drone large enough to attack the lodge? And what type of explosive would he use? And would he use more than one? For such a small location, one might be enough.

But he was also a sniper. Would he do that? Was there an explosive he could fire from a sniper's rifle?

This was all new to Mitch. He had no answers, no experience even to form a specific idea. And Bracken would have to deal with extremely tight security which had to be already forming at the lodge.

Wait! This was Saturday. Danny worked security on Saturdays at the *Center Stage* offices. He was an experienced security guy working several places, even went to Washington with his boss to meet with the feds. He should understand this type of situation. And the last time they talked he had…oh no…discussed nuclear back packs.

"Please, God, no," Mitch whispered. "Don't let Wilmer have a nuclear back pack."

He clicked on his Uber app and typed in *Center Stage*'s address.

On his way to the offices, he wondered about Wilmer Bracken's memory. He thought about how CIA agents lie to manipulate. He thought about how he had met both Bracken and Rebel by chance at McDonald's. Only with Rebel it had been chance, but she had recognized him and manipulated the situation, then later admitted it. He had thought earlier about whether Bracken had set up their meeting, but wrote that off, considering his memory problems. But what if he really didn't have memory problems? What if he was lying both in person and in his memoir?

Mitch breathed out in frustration. Hell. Right now he didn't know what to believe.

As Mitch reached the security desk, Danny was smiling at him.

"Mitch, my man, you look nervous and in a hurry. You got a news deadline on Saturday? Or are you upset about all the crap with Russia and China?"

"Danny, this crap with Russia and China has given me a great idea for a novel. I need to write it down before it gets away from me. And I need your help on understanding security so I can write about it."

"Whoa! You gonna give me a co-authorship?"

"How about just a dedication at the front of the book?"

"Count me in!"

"Great! Did you hear that, as a result of the Russia and China conflicts, that the Bilderberg Group has a special committee meeting Monday?"

"I heard the UN Security Council's meeting."

"Yeah, but the news said today that about 50 members of the Bilderbergs are going to meet at Lake Placid."

"The Bilderbergs. That's that group of big money guys that meet in secret every year?"

"Yeah. Here's what I'm thinking. I'm thinking an assassin goes to Lake Placid where they're meeting. What would he do?"

"He a foreign guy or an American?"

"American. I figure he's in intelligence."

"You mean he's working for the government or he's gone rogue?"

"He's gone rogue."

"FBI? CIA? NSA? Special Forces?"

"Probably CIA."

"Yeah, that'd be better. Covert shit."

"Yeah."

"He goes to Lake Placid?"

"Yeah, they're meeting at the Lake Placid Lodge. Great scenic shots if they make it into a movie."

"Good thinking. Big money in movies."

"I can use even little money. I'm a journalist."

"Ha! Okay. Lemme think. He wanna kill somebody in particular…or everybody?"

"Everybody. Fifty, maybe sixty people. Big brass folks: bankers, tech, weapons manufacturers, politicians."

"Whoa! That's a lotta brass! He's working alone?"

"Yeah. A lone wolf."

"Those meetings pay for a lot of security. They protect a broad area. Maybe five miles beyond the building where they meet, maybe more. They don't let anybody in."

"So…what can he carry and use effectively? Probably he'll get only one chance. So an explosive of some kind."

Danny leaned forward on the counter, thinking.

"Hmmm…maybe a shoulder-launched missile. You know, a bazooka. Or an RPG.

"What's that?"

"Rocket-propelled grenade. That doesn't sound powerful, but they've advanced weapons so much, and keep 'em secret, it could knock out 50 or 100 folks if they're clumped together. Maybe a smaller neutron bomb launched from an RPG."

"Neutron bomb? What's that?"

"It's designed so it doesn't destroy infrastructures, but will kill all the people. You might be able to launch a small one from a bazooka, if they've developed one. And knowing the military…"

"You talked to me last week about a nuclear back pack."

"Oh…yeah…ugh. You're talking explosive destruction and then radiation spreading. Bad shit."

"And it's portable?"

"Yeah. Easy to use it somewhere like Lake Placid. Used to be bulky and easy to spot. But this is the 2030s. Tactical nukes have become more streamlined. He could carry it in a van. Mount it on a shoulder launcher and he's in business."

"Is it easy to get possession of that kind of fire power?"

"If you're in the CIA, yeah."

"And if he's turned?"

"Oh, yeah. Weapons dealers ain't loyal to a country. They're loyal to money."

"And he'd have to penetrate really heavy security?"

"Really heavy. What he might want to do is find an elevated area outside the security zone, high enough where he could see the target."

"Could he use a drone?"

Danny thought about it.

"A drone. Yeah, I guess he could. A smaller drone. They got all sizes. Rapidly fly it over and past security. Maybe where they couldn't even see it until it's too late. Yeah."

"What if he was with the CIA and, like you said, turned? If the CIA knew he had turned, they'd follow him, right?"

"From the moment they learned he had turned. They'd try to grab him before he made it to Lake Placid. But if he made it, they'd be close on his trail."

Mitch thought a moment, then winked at Danny.

"Partner, you've saved me a ton of research. I'll note that in the dedication."

"You'd better," Danny smiled. As Mitch left, the guard called out, "Hey, and make sure the CIA guy gets laid before all this goes down!"

"Done!" called Mitch.

Head swimming, Mitch needed to get to another meeting. It would help him get centered and decide what he needed to do next regarding Bracken.

But he knew what he needed to do immediately about Rebel. He called her again. Only her voicemail.

"Dammit! Rebel…dammit!"

Mitch didn't even know if she had received his message.

The meeting calmed him some. Prayer helped. And the speaker offered a life story making clear that only a higher power could have helped him survive, then get sober.

The sun was setting as Mitch made his way home. He was suddenly craving a burger, and stopped in at the new Sin City burger fast-food in the Village. It seemed an appropriate name to fit what was going on with him. He got an Envy burger and fries to go.

More settled after eating, and not hearing from Rebel or Bracken, he decided to call Stan Hadley. He filled him in on his concerns.

"Maybe you should call the CIA," Hadley suggested.

"But what if they've got Bracken already? And would I endanger Miranda and the books by talking with them. Or myself. They questioned Rebel at her place, but they haven't been back to talk to me."

"But what if they don't have Bracken? And what if he's on his way to Lake Placid?"

"What if he's not?"

"What does your journalist's gut tell you?"

"That he is."

"And what does logic tell you about the damage he could do there? Do you want that on your conscience? And have you thought about its legal ramifications just on you alone?"

Silence.

"You know, there's a part of me that hates those moneygrubbers and warmongers as much as Bracken. The world would be better off if they didn't exist. But they do."

"And they have a legal right to their lives."

"But they don't have a legal right to take others' lives, which is what they do supporting these endless wars."

"Then, if they don't have a legal right, they should have to answer in court."

"You know better than that, Stan. You know the old saying: They're not only too big to fail, they're too big to jail. They just keep profiteering from war. That's what Bracken hates and what I hate."

"And what I hate. But this is a nation of laws, and I'm thinking that, if sober people like us decide not to follow the laws, we're dooming ourselves, and surely others."

Silence. Then Mitch:

"You know, Bracken likes to use the term 'conundrum', putting him at odds with himself. And that's where he is with the Constitution. On the one hand, he argues that the American citizen Anwar Al-Awlaki had Constitutional rights to be tried in court and not killed. But he doesn't see that for the bankers and techsters he wanted to kill. That's not consistent."

"Mitch…he may be in Lake Placid by now, or surely will be by morning."

"Why don't you go there and tackle him?"

"Would it were that simple."

Silence.

"One of the CIA guys that came to see me came back and left his business card in my door."

"You want me to call him. Say I represent you. That I'm defending your legal right as a journalist?"

"No. Fuck, no. I'll call him and assert my legal right as a journalist. And I won't mention the books."

"Call me after you talk with him."

"If I'm able to get him. Or get somebody. It's Saturday night."

Mitch got the card from his drawer and called the number. Of course, it was a recording. If the caller knows the extension or the name of the person he's calling…

"Officer Edward Madison," Mitch told the indifferent, mechanical voice. A computer clicked. A phone rang.

"Extension 428."

"Officer Edward Madison, please."

Silence. Then:

"Who's calling please?"

"Mitchell Morgan. I'm a journalist."

"What does this regard?"

"Is this Officer Madison?"

"No."

"Well, tell him my name. He'll know what it regards."

Silence.

"One moment."

Thirty seconds seemed like a bad year. Then, another voice.

"Mr. Morgan, Officer Madison isn't available. I'm Officer Roman Spinelli. Can I help you?"

"Maybe. Officer Madison left a business card in my door a couple of days ago, and I want to interview him."

"What about?"

"I wanted to ask him…I'm doing research on this emergency meeting of the Bilderberg Group that's about to take place in Lake Placid."

"Yes."

"You're aware of it?"

"Yes, it's been in the news."

"I wanted to ask Officer Madison if he has any information about a possible planned assassination attempt at that meeting."

Silence. Then:

"Have you heard of a possible planned assassination?"

"I've heard a rumor."

"Where did you hear this rumor?"

"I'm sorry, I can't reveal my source."

Silence.

"Who specifically is supposed to be killed?"

Silence.

"Everybody."

Silence.

"I understand. Mr. Morgan, I'll leave a message for Officer Madison."

"So, he'll be there later?"

Silence.

"I'll leave a message."

"My number is…"

"We have your number. Thank you for calling."

"You're welcome."

Click.

Heavy breathing. Then a whispered prayer. He called Stan.

"That was a pretty heady approach," Stan said.

"Following your and my discussion about legal rights, it seemed kinda logical. What any reasonable man would do in a similar situation."

Stan laughed softly.

"Yeah, if you're a journalist," the lawyer said. "Let's see if Madison calls you."

"If he's still alive. Let's see if they respond immediately by trying to prevent an assassination."

"It seems logical that they will. You know what?"

"What?"

"You might want to sleep somewhere besides at home tonight."

"You know what. You may be right."

Washington Square Hotel advertised itself as "105 feet from Washington Square Park", with WiFi. Mitch in the past had reserved the quaint rooms there for visiting friends. Tonight he lay in the twin bed under the framed photo portrait of Clark Gable, unable to sleep.

Internal voices kept shouting questions. Why wasn't Rebel calling him? Where the hell was Bracken? What about Miranda? Should he take her job offer? Why shouldn't he? What about the forewords she wanted for the two books? What would he write? Would the CIA come after him?

It all got to be too much. He slid from under the covers, kneeling beside the bed, his sweaty hands folded in prayer.

He whispered: "Please, Great Spirit, guide us. Grant us your calming, healing sleep."

He deep-breathed. Crawled back in bed. He began repeating the brief prayer as a mantra. And sleep came.

A LOST SMARTPHONE

Sunday morning the temperature had started to rise into the 40s. Mitch checked on temperatures at Lake Placid. Still below 30. Ah, April in New York. Not like April in Paris, which would be nice, maybe even with the climate change.

On first waking, Mitch had tried again to call Rebel. No response. Nothing from Bracken. Nothing from the CIA.

He checked the news. Nothing about Lake Placid.

He hit a morning meeting, then went for breakfast back at the Quantum Leap. He poured over *The New York Times* as he chewed on an omelet and pancakes again.

Fighting was continuing in the Arctic and was more sporadic in the South China Sea. The UN Security Council was meeting at 10 am, just an hour from now.

Mitch found an article about the planned Bilderberg special meeting. It listed the top executives already beginning to arrive there Saturday night, and all the big names expected to have convened by Monday:

Chairmen of the largest banks in the U.S.: JPMorgan Chase, Citigroup, Bank of America, Wells Fargo, Goldman Saks, Morgan Stanley. Those six alone with $20 Trillion in assets. At least six more major banks would be joining them.

Then there were the major weapons manufacturers the banks helped fund: Raytheon, Boeing, Lockheed Martin, General Dynamics, Northrop Grumman. Those five alone supplying $300 Billion worth of murderous mechanisms ranging from hand weapons to missiles to ships and jets to neutron and nuclear devices. Every year.

And to complete -- to borrow from George W. Bush, the "axis of evil" -- Big Tech that supplied the vast technology for everything from computers for defense systems to global surveillance: Amazon, Alphabet (parent of Google), Microsoft, and Oracle. Together those tech corporations were worth $8 Trillion.

Mitch began thinking about all those corporate chiefs gathered in one area. About some type of explosion ending all their lives. About the effects on their companies, on the stock market, on the global economy. And include the President of the United States, Canada's Prime Minister, Mexico's president. And the Prime Minister of Great Britain and President of France were also listed as planning to attend.

What would all this mean as military conflict seemed to be growing? Mitch saw an article that North Korea had just attacked South Korea late Saturday.

If the CIA did not have Bracken, if he was indeed going to or in Lake Placid, if the CIA or others weren't able to stop him, and if he succeeded in a massive assassination of Western leaders…would that allow Russia and China to…

Suddenly his appetite was gone. He paid his check and left his meal half-eaten.

Doris, the sweet waitress who saw him so often he felt like a friend, came up.

"Mitch, are you alright?"

"I've…I've got a lot going on, Doris. Thanks for asking. Gotta get to work."

And he was gone.

Back at his apartment, no one was waiting. No business card left. He got on his PC. He needed to try and start writing the book forewords Miranda had requested.

Nothing was coming. He closed his eyes, deep breathing, whispering a prayer.

The smartphone beckoned. It was Rebel!

"Hey, babe. Checking in."

"Where the hell have you been? I've been calling."

189

"Oh…I'm sorry. I lost my…fucking phone. We were out shooting, and through all our moving around, it slipped out of my bag. It's lying somewhere in the frozen Adirondacks. I just got a disposable cell phone. Until I can…"

"Rebel, you've got to get away from the lodge! You've even got to get out of Lake Placid!"

"What? What's going on? As a matter of fact, we got suddenly forced out of the lodge. Some kind of big emergency meeting, they said. I'm in a motel on the edge of town now."

"It's dangerous there! Very dangerous! A possible attack on that emergency meeting!"

"Mitchell!?! I can't just leave. We've got a shoot in a few minutes. And our last shoot early tomorrow morning."

"Where will that be?"

"Both of them somewhere away from town. They've got security swarming all over the place. They won't let us go anywhere in town or near the lodge."

"Good! Your last shoot? Then you'll come home?"

"Yes. I'll probably be on the train tomorrow afternoon."

Mitch breathed out heavily.

"Okay…good…good…"

"Mitchell? Are you okay?"

"I'm just worried about you. And your crew. All hell could break loose up there."

"Well, the hellers will have a helluva lot to contend with if they try anything. It's like a whole army up here defending this place now."

"Okay. Good…Rebel…"

"Yes?"

"Come home."

"I'll be back tomorrow night. Can't wait to hug you…and maybe play around a little!"

Mitch let out a nervous laugh.

"Here's a kiss to calm you down."

She let out a smooch.

"Thank you," he said softly.

"Love you, Mitchell Morgan."

"Love you, Rebel Daley."

She was off the phone.

Nothing like praying to a higher power and then hearing from the woman you love to calm and center a shaky journalist. Mitch could write now.

He started first with a foreword for the nuclear-weapons report. That would be a good warmup to prepare him for the Bracken memoir's foreword.

In the winter of 2030, somehow a U.S. top-secret government document appeared briefly online: an executive summary for the President and other high officials. It was a 45-page introduction to a detailed analysis of every foreign government's nuclear weapons program.

I stumbled on the summary purely by chance. My natural journalist's response was to make a copy so I could study it. I printed a copy of it. By the time I had retrieved it from the copier room and returned to my desk, the document had disappeared from the Internet.

It's still not clear who had placed the document online, or who removed it. What is clear: this document, a part of a larger study paid for by American taxpayers' dollars, was on a deadly subject that can affect the existence of civilization. The public deserves to be made aware of it. That is why Soule Books has published it.

Mitch would keep it brief from there, including a short paragraph explaining the founding and mission of Soule Books. Then he decided to take a break, clicking on the afternoon Mets game against the Philadelphia Phillies.

But he kept thinking about Rebel being in Lake Placid. He probably wouldn't be relieved until she walked in the door and he could hold her.

And he was thinking about Bracken. Was he around Lake Placid now? Did the CIA have him in New York? Had Mitch done the right thing by calling the CIA? Yes, he believed he did, especially the way he approached it. If Officer Spinelli worked at all with Madison, he would probably have known who Mitch was when he called. If Bracken had killed Madison and Gonzalez, Spinelli surely would know who Mitch was. And he definitely would understand what Mitch was alluding to by suggesting an assassination of everybody.

The previous restless night, the moving through freezing weather today, and the constant stress he was under found Mitch exhausted in only mid-afternoon. He closed his eyes to simply deep-breathe and relax. But sleep can be a relentless foe, and won out.

When he woke, it was dark. He checked the time. 8:25. He thought about Miranda. He should update her on Bracken.

But first, he wanted to think about responding to her job offer. It didn't take long. Fresh from a rest, he was thinking clearly. Like her, he had gotten sober to be of service somehow. For years now, it had been as a journalist reporting on humans making their living on stage, film, radio, and TV. He'd done that long enough.

If somebody wrote his obit after this life was done, what would he want them to say? That he had spent his best years writing about the entertainment industry? Or would he want them to report that he had served people well by braving the fight against corrupt business and government. By working with and supporting whistleblowers, and presenting accurate, detailed books to the public that deserved to know.

Miranda had now offered him this chance. And they could fulfill that mission as a team. "Yea, team!" she had quipped. He laughed out loud, feeling her humor and enthusiasm.

She seemed to still hold that enthusiasm as she answered the phone. "Hey, Mitch!"

"Well, don't you sound like one chipper New Yorker!"

"How are you doing on the forewords?"

"I've finished the one for the nuke report. And I'm circling the prey for the memoir."

"Excellent! Well, let me share with you that I just returned about an hour ago from a meeting that can help us move forward with Soule Books!"

"Music to my ears. Say more."

"I talked with two old friends, folks with money looking for investments to help them with their taxes."

"And that would be us?"

"Us, you say? Yes sir! Us! Are you in?"

"If you've found the money, I'm in."

"That's one thing I wanted to share! This meeting included finding you money. And Eureka!"

"You know what I say to that?"

"What?"

"Yea, team."

They both laughed.

Then Mitch updated her on his experience over the last two days. Miranda listened intently.

"But you don't know if he's in Lake Placid?"

"I don't know where he is. And I wasn't about to ask the CIA. At least, not yet."

"That was a pretty cool approach you used with them."

"I think I was being guided."

"I concur. So, what's next?"

"Well, the Bilderbergs are gathering as we speak. They're officially to meet tomorrow. No one knows the schedule except them. I'm figuring they'll have a big meeting in the morning. Probably break for lunch, have their little meetings, then reconvene in the afternoon for a final resolution of what actions they'll take."

"You've got bankers, tech people, weapons makers, and politicians," Miranda said. "Sounds like the people who make war, not prevent it."

"You've been reading my mail."

Miranda let out a sigh. Then:

"Well…I've got a big day tomorrow trying to keep a publishing business going while funding a startup. I'm sneaking toward the bedroom."

"Sleep well, teammate."

"Talk tomorrow?"

"Concur. Love, Bless, and Bye!"

"Bye."

ENDGAME

Monday morning, Mitch woke, looked at his phone. No message from Rebel. She had probably already risen at dawn and left for the last day's morning shoot. He sat to look quickly at Facebook before leaving for work. To his surprise, he saw a private message on Messenger from Rebel. He clicked to the page. She had sent him a video-and-voice clip.

Mitch switched on it to see Rebel's splendid face, smiling. She began softly singing a Capella:

The way you wear your hat

The way you sip your tea

The memory of all that

No, they can't take that away from me ...

She sang the entire song, her voice growing louder on that one line:

The way you changed my life ...

Then at song's end, she gazed into the camera, face moving closer to the lens.

"I'm off to work, babe. Didn't want to wake you by calling. So decided to serenade you instead. Love you."

She leaned back, blew him a kiss. Gave a small giggle, and signed off.

Mitch decided to try texting Bracken again. No response. He called. Nothing.

At work, Mitch was forcing himself to push through the trade paper's Monday as he thought about Rebel and Bracken...and the Bilderbergs. At his PC, he would put stories in the "buckets", switch windows to work on his column, then change to another window where he had tuned into CNN's website news reports.

He had emailed Miranda the foreword to the nuclear-weapons report. In his note, he explained to her he hadn't been able to finish the longer foreword for Bracken's memoir, but hoped to tonight.

She emailed back a funny GIF: an animation of an old photo of Carl Bernstein and Bob Woodward, the two *Washington Post* reporters famous for taking down President Nixon with their Watergate stories. They were both dancing and giving a thumbs up.

Her message was clear. He wondered if he and Miranda could have a similar impact with Soule Books. Time and the higher power would tell.

11 a.m.

Mitch switched to the CNN window right as the anchor was saying lightly, "…and we now have Blake Simmons reporting from what appears to be his new home! Lake Placid, New York. Blake?"

Simmons was no longer standing behind Lake Placid Lodge. He was all the way across the lake, the old building small but visible behind him in the distance. He wasn't smiling.

"And what a nice home this would be, Linda. But today security is keeping us a safe distance from the world's chiefs of finance, tech, and politics meeting right over there. Word is that the group of some 50 or 60 titans had convened this morning to discuss how to respond to the growing conflicts of the United States with Russia and China. And other conflicts seem to be rising as a result. With not only North and South Korea. But now Israel and Iran, increasing skirmishes which can be just as threatening as the global powers' struggles.

"Meanwhile, here in Lake Placid, a problem seems to have arisen…"

Mitch's phone rang.

"Mitchell Morgan."

Rebel seemed ecstatic.

"Hey, love! I'm done with the shoot! I'm at the train station! On my way to you!"

"Oh, babe, that's great! Hold on a second, will you?"

Mitch looked at the CNN screen. Simmons was continuing:

"The Bilderberg group reportedly were to follow their open meeting with lunch, then an afternoon session to close out. But now we've received a report that the lunch and later session have been cancelled for security reasons…"

"Mitchell?"

"Honey, CNN's at Lake Placid. There's a problem with the Bilderberg meeting."

"You think it's the danger you were telling me about?"

"Hold on."

Simmons:

"…that there has been growing concerns of some type of attack planned on this distinguished gathering. Federal authorities appear to be taking every precaution to see that doesn't happen. We'll be checking with…"

A bright flash on screen. The CNN picture flickered…then went blank. Simmons' voice garbled…then went silent.

"Mitchell?" Rebel's voice was soft, curious. "There's been some type of terribly bright flash outside…I can't tell wha…" A brief shrill sound like a crow's call. Then silence.

Mitch's body surged with heat, now suddenly shaking, his heart pounding.

"Rebel!...Rebel!!"

No sound.

"No! No no no no no!"

Mitch was suddenly standing, legs moving, his psyche seeming to want some place to run to. But there was no place. No way to help Rebel.

On the screen, the scene had switched back to the anchor showing confusion and an attempt to remain calm.

"We seem to have some technical problem at Lake Placid. We'll try to get back with Blake Simmons…and keep you updated on activity there…Meanwhile, here's more on the U.S. conflicts…"

Mitch was whispering desperately into the phone.

"Rebel! Rebel! Oh…please, God…no…"

His body went limp, falling into his chair.

"Hey, Mitch, did you look at my story on..."

Mindy Watson, the Broadway theater editor, was standing behind Mitch. She stopped abruptly, gazing at him.

He was slumped over at his desk, crying, knowing what the whole world soon would know.

AFTERMATH

The Tactical Nuclear Weapon (TNW) used on Lake Placid Lodge had been small enough to fire from a shoulder bazooka, but powerful enough to destroy the lodge and the village, including the train station a few miles away. Radiation would further infect any living being within a farther range.

The U.S. government announced its investigations were revealing that the attack had been probably by a single person: a foreign agent, either from Russia, China, or North Korea. With possible cooperation by all three. Washington's analysis was the perfect formula which could lead to world war.

The nation's new president, a shade more liberal than the assassinated woman he had replaced, alleged the investigation was continuing. He vowed to work for peace with the leaders of the countries just accused of the attack.

Since the federal government didn't want to acknowledge Bracken, it appeared they would not engage Mitch in any way for his connection to the former agent. Yet.

Following the Lake Placid bombing, Mitch gave his two weeks notice at *Center Stage*, then moved on to work with Miranda and Soule Books, which had published both Bracken's manuscripts just days after the historic bombing.

In his foreword to Bracken's memoir, Mitch traced his meeting and relationship with Bracken. He briefly covered Bracken's background, and analyzed him and possible reasons for his actions, including his belief that Bracken had been responsible for the Lake Placid bombing. He also believed that, after the memoir was published and the public read it, the U.S. government would have to make known the truths of their investigation, including Bracken's guilt.

He included in his foreword that one victim of the Lake Placid bombing had been Rebel Daley, a professional model he had grown to love, and missed terribly.

He did not write how each evening he would return to his lonely apartment, and at some time every night couldn't help but get on his computer. He would go to his Facebook Messenger page, and call up his video-and-sound message of the beautiful Rebel smiling, singing only to him.

ABOUT THE AUTHOR

Roger Armbrust

Roger Armbrust's decades of journalistic experience include being a national news editor and managing editor in New York, where he also taught a professional writing course at New York University. His poems have appeared in New York Quarterly, Chelsea, Icarus, and Delaware Poetry Review. He has 16 published books including two novels, a creative philosophy memoir, a collection of political and economic columns, and several volumes of poetry. He now lives in his hometown of Little Rock, Arkansas.

BOOKS BY THIS AUTHOR

<u>**Pressing Freedom, A Novel**</u>

Go Deep. Take Chances.: Embracing the Muse and Creative Writing

The Vital Realities for 2020 and Beyond

Writings on Water Wars, Nuclear Devastation, Endless War, Economic Revolution, and Surveillance versus Freedom

The Aesthetic Astronaut: Sonnets

Oh, Touch Me There: Love Sonnets

Mending Torn Pages: Sonnets

Maestro: Love Sonnets

I Write This to You: Sonnets

Walked Through Storm to You: Love Sonnets

Poems While We Dream: Sonnets and Songs

Before It All Ends: Breathless Sonnets

All Things at Once: Sonnets and Songs

The Last Quiet Place on Earth: Sonnets in the Time of Coronavirus

We Who Battle Demons: Sober Sonnets

How to Survive: Poems

Final Grace: A Sad Tale

Made in the USA
Columbia, SC
09 June 2025

59154378R00115